The Elitists

JOSEPH MENSER

First published by Dog Ear Publishing
4011 Vincennes Rd
Indianapolis, IN 46268
www.dogearpublishing.net

ISBN: 978-1-4575-4438-5

This book is printed on acid-free paper.

Printed in the United States of America

Introduction

2019 was the year of World War III. The United Nations confronted North Korea regarding its stockpile of chemical explosives. Countries flooded to North Korea to defeat this nation and free its citizens. North Korea was aware of the front heading their way and launched their chemical missiles all over the world. The gas was clear with no smell. When inhaled, the gas made breathing feel as if there were glass shards in the victim's throat and eventually shut down the respiratory system. One breath of the gas was fatal, and the individual died in a matter of minutes.

The missiles landed throughout every country except the United States. Navy men shot down the missiles heading east from North Korea, causing the gas to explode on them. In doing so, they saved the United States and lower parts of Canada. The gas expanded on the ground wiping out entire continents of people. North Korea did not predict the length of time the gas would be in the air. The gas stayed on the surface level of the earth for weeks, killing almost everyone in Asia, Europe, Australia, Africa, Central America, and South America. The only place that held life was the United States. Communication outside North America completely stopped. No messages were received after this day.

The United States sent airplanes across the seas to check for any survivors, but no plane ever made it home. The United States started to learn that the gas rose to the upper atmospheres and stayed there. This did not affect sunlight or crops, but the United States learned the gas was corrosive to metals, which caused planes to stall and crash. The gas slowly took over the entire atmosphere, and the United States skies were engulfed in this gas. Planes were now useless. Helicopters continued to be used, because they flew low enough to remain unaffected by the gas. The United States was the last safe place in the world to live but tensions grew within the country over the years.

In the year 2033, an American Civil War broke out between the economic classes of society. The government was forced to cancel all welfare and government-aided assistance programs due to the overpopulation of the nation and the massive debt it had piled up in hopes of keeping citizens afloat. After cancelling all the programs, the lower class revolted and launched aggressive protests against successful businesses and cities throughout the nation.

Planning to reduce the threats of the lower class, the government called for the Second Amendment to be cancelled. Anyone caught possessing a firearm while not in uniform was considered an active threat. Representatives of government agencies could respond in any form that the individual felt was necessary. The result of this was extremely troublesome to the United States, and an underground government named The Madison Legacy emerged. James Madison was known as, "The Father of the Bill of Rights". For this reason, guerilla warfare forces chose to be named the Madison Legacy. They felt their rights were no longer protected or respected.

The Madison Legacy was formed of mostly lower-class citizens and anyone else who felt repressed by the United States government. The Madison Legacy sporadically bombed the United States with plans to overrun their politics and replace them with their own. Unfortunately, for the Madison Legacy, they lacked the technology and war equipment needed to take over any significant landmarks, but they were still strong enough to split from the United States.

In the year 2044, the land of North America was split into the Madison Legacy and the United States. The two nations signed a ceasefire in 2044 as well, in hopes of keeping the land intact as much as they could. The United States realized they could no longer unite the states and eliminate the differences.

The Madison Legacy and the United States both claimed their territories and built walls to signify and protect their citizens from one another. To save resources and to avoid spreading their armies too thin, portions of North America were left unclaimed. These areas were inhabited by civilians who had not taken a side in the war, had an unwillingness to move, or wanted a safety tactic from attacks from either side of the war. Civilians in the unclaimed territories were given the nickname, the Outliers.

The Outliers generally sided with the Madison Legacy in terms of policies, and in the event another war arose, they would fight alongside the Madison Legacy. This was what the United States feared and needed to stop.

In response, the United States formed a special operations team under the name, the Elitists. The mission of the Elitists was to neutralize any potential threats that could harm the United States or join the Madison Legacy. The Elitists consisted of six squad members who were the top of their class in weaponry, combat fighting, and war tactics.

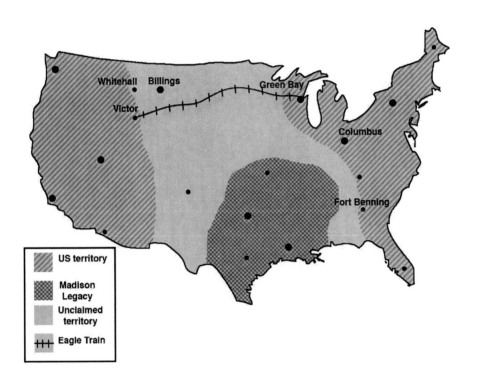

CHAPTER 1

Opportunity   *May 1, 2046*

G reen Bay, Wisconsin to the City of Victor, Idaho. Normally this would
  not be an ideal train ride, but due to the war, this was the main source
of traveling. The train was named, The Eagle. The Eagle traveled between the
two main ports left in the United States. At these ports, trade occurred between
the west and east portions of the United States.

The Madison Legacy revolution left the North American continent in
social ruins and left large portions of the country unclaimed. The United States
felt the need to consolidate their forces and supplies to the Atlantic and Pacific
coasts. The Madison Legacy had similar ideas and headed south claiming the
Gulf of Mexico for itself.

After the walls were built to protect the citizens of each nation, more than
800,000 square miles of North American property was left unclaimed. In this
unclaimed territory, individuals known as Outliers lived, because either they
hated both nations or they had an unwillingness to move from their homeland.
Cities emerged as people colonized in the forgotten land. The area offered
enough fresh water and animals for food to still be habitable to these people.

In the signed agreement between the Madison Legacy and the United
States, there were to be no more battles between the two, and they would coex-
ist in the continent. This peace applied to all people living within the countries'
boundaries. A man named Marshall was soon to see the secrets behind his
beloved nation of the United States.

Marshall was a twenty-seven-year-old United States Marine Scout Sniper
who graduated from his sniper academy three years prior at the top of his class
at Fort Benning, Georgia. Marshall had been on east wall duties for the past
three years to protect his people from any Madison Legacy bombing or shoot-
ings. Marshall had been in combat before and was extraordinarily efficient with
assault rifles, hand-to-hand combat, and, most importantly, his M26.

The M26 was a lightweight version of the M24 model commonly used by
United States snipers in the early 2020s. The M26 featured a distance measure within
the scope allowing a faster-paced sighting and less reliability on the team's spotter.

He was considered a hero in the battle of New Orleans of 2042. He recorded eighteen confirmed sniper kills that week, while earning twelve confirmed close combat kills. This was the reason Marshall was chosen for the Elitist program.

Marshall received a notice while preparing for his shift on wall duty. A mail runner handed him a letter and told him, "It's of the upmost importance you respond to this letter."

Marshall sat down, opened the letter, and immediately noticed it was signed by General Quartz, Leader of the United States Militia. Marshall began reading and realized it was an invitation to meet with General Quartz in Columbus, Ohio. The letter spoke of a mission that needed Marshall's skills for success.

Marshall immediately informed the acting Captain of his outpost and the Captain let Marshall leave at the end of his shift. While Marshall walked to his home within the outpost, a van pulled up to Marshall and a man on the inside called out, "We've retrieved all your items from your home, and we're ready for the drive up to Columbus whenever you are."

Marshall became a tad concerned over the pushiness of the situation, but Marshall was a firm believer in the order of power in the army. He listened to the man and got into the van.

No one talked for the entirety of the ride thus far and Marshall became even more concerned about where he was heading. He attempted to make small talk.

"Any of you guys see the game between Georgia and South Carolina?"

"I'm sorry, Sir, we're not allowed to speak to you due to the privacy of this mission," stated one of the Soldiers sitting next to him.

"Understood," said Marshall, but in reality, nothing was understood, and he started to worry for his safety. He remembered he did not say goodbye to his friends and had no idea of how long he would be gone. Marshall tried to rest, because there was nothing he could do at this moment so there was no need to stress.

Several hours later, the van arrived with two Soldiers waiting at the gates to escort Marshall inside the facility.

"Sir, I need you wake up. We made it to Columbus and the General's on a tight schedule," said the Soldier sitting next to him.

"Of course, of course," Marshall said as he gathered his things and exited the van.

Marshall walked over to the two guards at the door and promptly told him, "You can leave your stuff here, and someone will put it in your bunk. We have to get you to the General."

Marshall did as he was told and hopped on a small AV. Marshall made it to the front of the building, walked in, and continued following his escorts. They pointed him to a room where one of the guards walked in and let General Quartz know Marshall was there. Marshall was allowed to enter and once doing so, saluted General Quartz.

"At ease, at ease, my friend," said General Quartz, calmly and welcoming.

"I'm very happy you made the choice to accept my invitation."

"Of course, Sir. Anything I can do to help, count me in," said Marshall anxiously.

"That's the exact reason why I want you to be assigned to my team on a mission the United States is undertaking. I've read everything there's to know about you and have seen your impressive shooting in person at practice. You're not afraid to make the tough calls. You are exactly the Soldier I need to complete this mission,"

"Well, thank you, Sir," said Marshall. Marshall was getting a little frustrated because he still did not know anything about this so-called mission and was worried what they may ask of him.

"I also know about the incident in 2033 when your mom died in that train bombing. This is another reason why I want you on my team," said the General compassionately.

"You hate those filthy fucking inbreeds more than anyone I looked into."

"Yes, Sir," Marshall stated in a serious tone and started to gaze off with his eyes.

He then reminisced about the Madison Legacy bombing the train he was on that killed his mother. This was the start of his hatred toward the Madison Legacy and was why he joined the army in the first place. He felt the need to avenge his mother's death, as she was the only family member in his life.

"Well, I have some insider information that another war could be brewing between the two of us, and we'll not be caught off guard this time," said General Quartz.

"I've set up a specialist team near former Billings, Montana. I want you to join my team. You're one of the best snipers in the United States and your country needs you right now," pleaded the General.

"I'll happily accept any mission the United States gives me, but I'd prefer some more information about what my job entails."

"Of course, of course. You will be sniper over-watch of a team of six. The other five members have been chosen already by the Captain, who's involved tremendously with this project."

"I don't mean to pry, Sir, but why Billings, Montana?"

"Ask as many questions as you desire, Marshall. Don't hesitate at all toward me. Billings is a rundown city in the middle of nowhere, where the six of you can train in urban warfare. Putting you in the Outliers will keep tensions down within our walls and will hide our plans from Madison," said General Quartz.

"I accept this mission, Sir, when do I leave?"

"I knew you were the right Soldier," said General Quartz with an enormous smile on his face.

"When do I depart?"

"I need you to be on the Eagle by tomorrow morning at 8 AM. That's the next trip to West U.S. 45.7867° N, 108.5372° W, which are the coordinates to Billings. I'll be giving you a cell phone with this information on it tomorrow. I know cell phones have been gone for a while now but they're needed on this mission. Our technology team created a solar-and movement-powered cell phone. Sunlight charges the cell phone and so does moving with the phone. I want you to plan to jump off the train near those coordinates to minimize your walking so you won't be late. Your Captain will be waiting for you in the area. You'll make contact with him and will then follow orders straight from him."

Marshall felt a tad nervous because he had not been on a train since the incident and had built anxiety toward trains. Despite his nervousness on the inside, Marshall showed pure confidence and determination on his exterior.

"I understand the mission, Sir."

"Fantastic news to hear, Marshall. I'm going to have one of the guards escort you to your bunk for the night, and you may call one person from home to let them know you'll be gone. But do not disclose any information beyond that point," said General Quartz in an increasingly strict tone.

"I don't need to call anyone, but I'll see you tomorrow to gear up and head out. Thank you for this opportunity," said Marshall gratefully.

"No, thank you, Marshall. We need more troops like you on the battlefield and the Madisons will no longer exist."

Marshall left the room with many questions about what was to come but was still ecstatic to be the one chosen for this mission. He was getting sick and tired of staring from the wall duty and needed a new job. Marshall was escorted to his room, where he found his stuff sitting there.

"We will be bringing you dinner to your room tonight, Sir. If you need anything please push this button, and a guard will be here immediately," explained the guard.

"I'm not allowed to leave?"

"I am sorry, Sir, but with the importance of this mission, we cannot allow any chance of a compromise. The General sends his apologies."

"No, it's fine, I'll be here all night," said Marshall.

The guard left his room, and Marshall immediately inspected his surroundings. It was a dark room with no windows but just one light, creating an eerie affect. It had a bed, desk, refrigerator with some food, and a bathroom.

He then wondered what his next mission would be if the training needed to be this secret. He headed toward his bed and laid down on his back staring at the ceiling. Marshall laid there awaiting the next journey of his life and drifted to sleep.

★ ★ ★

General Quartz reached for his phone as Marshall left the room after the agreement. He already had a message typed out saying, "Affirmative."

General Quartz sent the message, put the phone away, and pulled out a celebratory drink.

CHAPTER 2

The Eagle *May 2, 2046*

Marshall woke up at five in the morning and began his morning workout routine of pushups, crunches, and air-boxing. Marshall was a firm believer in staying constantly fit and aware of his surroundings. Marshall would never be caught off-guard with an enemy as long as he stuck to his beliefs.

The 6 AM hour arrived, and a guard knocked on Marshall's very secure door. "Are you ready to depart, Sir?"

Marshall looked around his room once more, making sure he had all of his belongings and replied, "Of course."

Marshall was escorted to a helicopter, which would take him to the Eagle where he met with General Quartz one last time.

"Glad to see you didn't run off last night," said General Quartz in a joking tone.

"The door was difficult to open," Marshall said quickly back to him.

"Well, I'm happy you're still in high spirits. I'm going to give you the rundown on what'll happen next on the train ride."

"I had some Soldiers sneak your weapons on the train. You'll head to the bathroom as you approach Billings. The weapons are hidden under the floor compartment. You'll then jump out of the bathroom window when you're close to Billings."

"Yes, Sir."

"Soldiers often travel on these trains, so you won't look out of place. Even having a pistol on your side is normal, but I can't have you walking around with an M26. That would look out of place," General Quartz said with laugh.

"Your phone will be constantly giving you your coordinates, and you can jump whenever you see it's beneficial. I repeat again, though, if you tell anyone about where you're heading, I will have you terminated along with whoever you spoke to," said General Quartz as his smile faded.

"I understand, Sir."

"Great. You're all set now then, Marshall. There's one number in your phone and it's to your Captain. Message him saying, "Down", when you make the drop, and his squad will make their way toward you as you do the same.

"I'll be seeing you in a few months, and I wish you the best of luck, Marshall. Remember: Hesitation kills," said General Quartz with one last laugh while exiting the helicopter.

Marshall gave one last mercy laugh to the General and was beyond confused on why this General had such a sense of humor for such a serious topic. General Quartz changed between hot and cold faster than Marshall could adjust to the conversation.

Marshall did not realize during his entire briefing the helicopter had landed. The General was escorted with several troops to a car that seemed to be heading for downtown Green Bay. Marshall was told to get into a separate car that would drive him the last few miles to the Eagle.

The guard in the passenger seat handed Marshall an M9 Berretta, the most common pistol used in the military due to the mass production of them in the 2020s. Marshall was quick on the trigger with this weapon, had a fast draw, and was an accurate shot.

Marshall was then handed a spring-loaded pocketknife named Aerial Air 760 for stealthy concealing and quick attacks. Marshall felt a lot more at home now that all of the talking was done and he had a weapon in his possession again. He hoped they took care of his sniper rifle and he did not have any major repairs when he got it back.

Marshall sat in the car looking at the massive wall in front of him that separated civilization from wasteland. He had not been on the outside of the walls since his battle in Louisiana, which was over three years ago now.

The wall stood one-hundred feet tall and stretched north to south on both West and East United States. There were hallways installed inside the wall and watchtowers were attached as well to prevent any surprise attacks. Marshall was more familiar than most with these walls due to his watch duties, but then he saw the opening where the train exited.

The Eagle was fifteen cars long, ten of which held supplies to travel back and forth such as water, food, and usually weaponry. The other five cars were used for Soldiers transporting between locations or lucky individuals who won the lottery and were selected to take the trip.

The car stopped and Marshall was aware this time and got out of the car. The guards gave him his ticket, backpack of supplies, and told Marshall, "Good luck, Sir, and thank you for your service to this country."

Marshall gave both of the guards a nod and headed toward the Eagle. Marshall had lived in military bases for the past ten years and realized how difficult some citizens had living here. The United States did its best to take care of their citizens, but some families just pulled the short straw in life and were born into poverty and illness.

Marshall arrived to a mass of people clogging the entry gate. He found himself standing next to another Soldier.

"You pulled west duty, too, huh?" asked the Soldier.

"Yeah."

"This is my second tour and honestly, it's pretty nice there so I think you'll like it. Less tension from the guys in charge in my opinion…"

The Soldier continued rambling toward Marshall while Marshall looked for a faster way onto the train. As Marshall looked around, a civilian ran up to him, began crying, and pulled on his uniform.

"Sir, please take my son!" exclaimed the man who was sobbing. The man then pointed to his baby boy, held by his mother, and saw she was crying, too.

"I can't take care of him. I don't have enough money to feed the people in my house. He's going to die if you don't take him!"

Marshall stared at the man not knowing what to say but felt his eyes begin to water. Marshall had learned to separate himself from emotion. That was a necessity as a Soldier. A Soldier was taught to view the enemy as a lesser being and not to feel disgust for killing a bug. Marshall could not apply his beliefs to this situation. Marshall had not dealt with this type of raw emotion since his mother passed away.

The Soldier to Marshall's right pushed the man away.

"Keep walking, you needy prick," said the Soldier in a disgusted tone.

"What're you doing!" exclaimed Marshall as he pushed the Soldier back.

"All these civilians are lazy and want handouts. That shit that just spoke to you probably hasn't worked in years and now wants you to take his baby because he can't even afford a condom. I'm surprised that guy could even get it up with a wife that looks like that," the Soldier said angrily.

Marshall had pure rage in his eyes and sucker punched the Soldier with a right hook to the Soldier's jaw. The Soldier immediately dropped to the ground unconscious. Marshall knew he had to protect his country but never thought he would have to punch one of his own to do so.

Madness started to erupt as civilians saw the Soldier laying on the ground. One man saw the pistol that was strapped to the unconscious Soldier's side. The man walked toward the pistol as Marshall walked toward the family with the baby.

"I'm sorry for that man's behavior, and I wish you the best of luck with your future. But I can't take your baby. The baby shouldn't suffer because you can't provide for him," said Marshall sternly.

Marshall grabbed his wallet from his back pocket and handed the man all the cash he had. The man hugged him aggressively, and Marshall smiled but then heard a gunshot.

Marshall immediately ducked pulling the father down with him, looking for where the shot had occurred. He saw it was a homeless man who stole the gun from the fallen Soldier. The crowd scattered in different directions, and Marshall saw the unconscious Soldier's head get trampled. He stood there for a moment trying to process he may have been the reason the Soldier was dead.

Marshall went directly into fight mode and saw the train started moving due to the gunfire. Marshall ran toward the train and continued to hear pistol shots. The homeless man was firing at the watchtower where a sniper was positioned. Marshall flashed his ticket to a fellow Soldier who had his head down and the Soldier examined it quickly.

"You better run, brother," the Soldier said.

Marshall did just that. He ran and hopped on the side of car thirteen, hugging the car tightly so he could fit through the tunnel leading to the Outliers. As he left the darkness of the tunnel Marshall looked up and saw the sniper taking aim at the homeless man and saw him fire.

The train was picking up speed, so Marshall knew he had to get inside quickly. He pried the window he was holding, into an open position and entered the car. This car had tons of canned food. Marshall felt disgusted with how much the United States was hoarding when they could be feeding any one of those families out there.

The front five cars were where people stayed, which meant Marshall had some walking to do to get to the front. As he approached car five, a woman opened the door for him.

"I see you had a tough ride so far," she said with a smile.

Marshall just smiled back at her.

"Well, I can take you to a seat unless you like rooming with the canned foods more."

"No, a seat would be great," said Marshall.

"Not many Soldiers made it on because of the early departure, so you can have your own private car if you'd like."

"That sounds great, let's do that," said Marshall.

"My name's Ariel by the way. If you need anything throughout your trip, let me know."

Ariel then led Marshall to car two, which was perfect for him because it had the bathroom where his supplies were hidden. Marshall sat down, and Ariel left the car telling him she would be right back with something to drink. Marshall started to worry because now he was the only one in the car, it would be noticeable when he jumped out and was not there anymore.

Before he could figure out a plan, he processed what just happened at the train station. He tried to rationalize with himself that what he did was unavoidable. Marshall kept debating whether he should have or should not have punched the Soldier. Every second he contemplated the situation, he came back to the realization that the horrid Soldier would have devastating effects on this country in the long run. That baby could cure a disease or negotiate the war but that Soldier would only amount to killing and offending without a cause. Marshall negotiated with his guilt and concluded the Soldier's life was a lost cause. That man deserved to be punched. What followed seemed to be a way the world was bettering itself.

During all of this thought, Ariel returned.

"Here's a nice glass of water for you," she said as she handed it to him.

Marshall gave a nod as Ariel sat down across from Marshall.

"I hope you don't mind," said Ariel with a smile on her face.

"You see I'm assigned this car, and it's just you tonight, so I'm kind of on vacation for this trip. What's your name and where're you from?" asked Ariel.

Marshall was not the kind of man to share personal small talk with someone he had just met. This was an odd situation for Marshall to be in, and he seemed nervous and frightened on the exterior. This was rare for him.

"What's wrong?" asked Ariel with a concerned look on her face.

"I don't like trains," Marshall said with a smirk.

"I think trains are so very relaxing, and I just feel luxurious to be in one," replied Ariel.

"Let's just say I've had a bad experience."

"What happened?"

Internally Marshall was beginning to fill with anger, because he did not ask her to sit down and ask him about his personal life. On the other hand, Marshall did find this girl sweet and figured he had a long train ride and did not need it to be awkward.

Marshall asked, "How old are you?"

"Oh, I am twenty. How old are you?"

"I turned twenty-seven last month, so I'm guessing you didn't hear about the Chicago train bombing of 2033 then…," said Marshall with a depressing tone.

"I don't know too much detail about it, but…were you on that train?"

"Yeah…my mom stood up to get me a drink and left for another car. That's when the Madison's bomb went off, killing everyone in the cars in front me. She was in the wrong place at the wrong time,"

"Oh my God, I'm so sorry," exclaimed Ariel. "I understand why you're nervous but this is my sixth trip, and this is a very sturdy train so you shouldn't worry," she added.

"Oh, I know. Thank you for your concern," said Marshall.

"Is that why you joined the army?"

"Yeah."

"My dad's in the army and told me I needed to get a job and stop living at home. So, this job works perfectly for me!"

Marshall realized the differences between the experiences the both of them have lived. Marshall started to like this girl though. He had been all business for so long and it was nice to have a conversation about life. He forgot all about these kind of experiences. Marshall felt odd but wanted to continue the conversation, so he asked her a question.

"What kind of job is your dream job?"

Ariel looked relieved Marshall was finally talking to her. Now she did not have to work so hard for a conversation.

"Well, in high school, we learned about the jetliners that carried people around the world but that dream isn't very likely anymore. So this job at least lets me travel," she said.

Marshall looked down at his feet in sadness. "Maybe in the next couple of years, the gas will clear out and we can fly again."

"Have you ever flown?" asked Ariel.

"I've been in a helicopter many times, but airplanes were banned long before I enrolled in the army. Another time the United States held their own against terrorists," Marshall said with a laugh.

"You weren't born yet, were you?" asked Ariel.

"No, I was born a couple months after the bombs went off in the world. My mom told me, though; it was the scariest moment of her life. All of the news stations told her to hide, and she waited to hear the sound of a bomb or the smell of the gas. My dad was stationed in Iraq, so he died from the bombings. My mom says she wouldn't be here if it wasn't for the United States," Marshall surprised himself with how much he was sharing.

"Why'd she say that?"

"They shot down all of the bombs heading east of Korea, which killed all the Navy personnel on the boats aiming the counter missiles. They saved millions of lives, though, and that's the reason we're on this train right now," Marshall said.

"Well, thank you for your service, Marshall. Your mom sounded like an amazing woman," said Ariel. Ariel did not feel comfortable with the silence after this serious conversation, so she decided to switch the subjects.

"Where're you headed in West U.S.?"

Fortunately, for Marshall, he had created a believable backup. He rehearsed it enough the previous night so it sounded truthful now.

"I was assigned a spot in California. I've never been there before, so it's going to be interesting."

Ariel's eyes immediately grew wide when she heard the word, "California."

"I have always wanted to see the Pacific Ocean," Ariel said in excitement.

"Well, I'll be just a short walk from the ocean."

"That's so amazing you get to go there!" Ariel said with enthusiasm. "I wish I had a reason to go there. Traveling is just so mesmerizing for me and there are so few places to go now…"

Marshall thought about what it would be like to have someone waiting for him when he returned from a day of work. These thoughts never crossed his mind before, because he had always focused on the current mission. What if he could just continue riding the train and get off in the West U.S. with Ariel? He had only been speaking to this girl for a few hours, but felt a connection he had never experienced.

"I was told I'll be getting a good-sized house over there, so feel free to stop by whenever," Marshall said extremely hesitantly.

Marshall actually felt nervous with this girl, which was surprising because he normally would not be choked-up for anyone or any event. Ariel, on the other hand, grinned with thoughts of traveling and getting to know Marshall a lot better.

"I'll most definitely take you up on that offer," Ariel said flirtatiously.

Marshall and Ariel continued talking into the night as the train continued heading west. Marshall had to use the bathroom and excused himself from Ariel. Meanwhile, Ariel headed toward the back of the train to get something to eat for the two of them. Marshall got to the bathroom and looked at himself in the mirror. Interestingly, he saw a genuine smile. He had not had a successful conversation with someone for far too long, and his body needed the social interaction.

As Marshall stood in the mirror looking at himself, he remembered his mission. The smile quickly left his face, and he dropped to the floor to make sure his gun bag was there. He removed the carpet and saw the trapdoor. Within the trap door compartment were two large bags: One with his rifle and one with supplies and other necessities. He checked his phone for his coordinates and realized he was just a couple of hours away.

The bathroom was the gateway to what life he would be deciding to take. Through the trap door was honor and a chance to destroy the Madisons. Through the bathroom door was Ariel and a chance at a normal life; one that could be shared with someone.

Marshall stared into the mirror thinking about what was to come over the next couple of hours. Marshall felt the train slow down, and he looked out the window to see the train was actually coming to a stop.

From training and experience, Marshall immediately readied himself for the worst. He looked to his right side where his pistol was loaded and ready to be fired. His hand levitated close to his sidearm while opening the bathroom door. A much older waitress than Ariel ran to the front of the train waving her hands. She was smiling and telling the Soldiers in the other cars everything was fine.

The waitress entered Marshall's car and said, "Stay calm Hon, probably just a maintenance check. Take a seat, and Ariel will be back soon with your drink."

Marshall did quite the opposite of what he was told. He looked through the windows on the back of the car to see if he could see Ariel, but he could not. Marshall walked to the front of the train and overheard some yelling.

"Do you three seriously get paid so little that we can't do one trip without some side-dealing?" exclaimed the older waitress. Marshall then heard a man's voice who he presumed was the conductor.

"Hey, you get your split, so I don't know why you're bitching," the conductor yelled back. Marshall opened the door in the front of his car and walked toward the back of the conductor's car. As he approached the back door, two large, fit men opened the conductor's door.

"Soldier, get back to your seat. You're not needed here," said one of the men.

"Why are we stopping?" asked Marshall.

"None of your business, Soldier. Now why don't you go sit down?"

The man moved closer to Marshall, doing his best to intimidate. The man stared into Marshall's eyes with his chest puffed out and a pissed-off look on his face.

"I have a job to do, so why don't you start the train and do yours," Marshall said with no hesitation.

"Oh, we have a tough guy here," the man said as the other goon behind him chuckled.

Marshall had already identified a knife in the front man's side pocket, and the man in the back had a sawed-off shotgun strapped on his back. He knew he could take both of them with ease and get the conductor to begin driving again. Right before Marshall was about to initiate his assault, Ariel opened the door behind him.

"Marshall, I got your drink for you, so why don't you come join me," she said with a smile. Marshall was torn between his natural urge to fight and his urge to be with Ariel. Marshall took one last look at the two men and walked backward to Ariel as she shut the door.

"What're they doing out there, Ariel?" Marshall asked with frustration in his voice.

"They trade supplies with some Outliers," she explained.

She pointed out the window and Marshall saw a large group of at least twenty people giving the two men money. The two men walked back to the conductor's car and hauled back large numbers of boxes.

"What do they trade?"

"Just the normal stuff. Food, water, weapons. They charge outrageous prices and the trading always ends up better for those on the train," said Ariel.

Outside was about fifty feet of dirt, which lead to a wall of trees, concealing the Outliers before they walked out toward the train. Marshall looked toward the top of the conductor's car through the window and saw the conductor standing on top of the train with a sniper rifle.

"They give the enemy guns?" asked Marshall with a pissed-off tone.

"And they pocket the money," said Ariel to finish Marshall's sentence.

"This is unacceptable. Don't other Soldiers care?"

"It's an unnecessary evil to confront these men. Most of the Soldiers don't want to die without a remembrance of valor. You wouldn't remember the death of a Soldier in the middle of the Outliers," said Ariel.

"People shouldn't fight for valor, they should fight for the right to sleep safely in a bed!" answered Marshall. "If the enemy is given weapons and ammo, I won't be sleeping easy tonight."

Marshall walked toward the front of his car and waited for the two men to return from their previous trip of deliveries.

"Hey look, this pussy is back," laughed one of the men.

Marshall recognized the situation and knew he had a sniper watching him. He figured he had only a few seconds to escape the line of fire. The man in front would charge for a fistfight. The man in back would take at least two seconds to swing the shotgun from his back to his front in a shooting position.

"You're providing weapons to an enemy of the U.S., which makes you an enemy to me," Marshall said calmly and sternly.

"Shut the fuck up, man," laughed the goon.

The front man was now only standing two feet away from Marshall on the train, with the goon with the shotgun roughly six feet away, standing in the dirt off the train. The sniper had his weapon down, just watching the argument in amusement from atop the conductor's car.

The front man lunged forward with a right hook as Marshall ducked. In the process of ducking, Marshall pulled his switchblade from his left side and the blade clicked open. Marshall stabbed the man in the heart. Marshall grabbed the front man's head with his left hand and pulled him closer. He preceded to swing his body to the left just in case the sniper was taking aim, and Marshall noticed the man in back had yet to pull his firearm.

Marshall then threw the limp body to the ground and ran into the conductor's car.

"What the fuck are you doing?" screamed the conductor.

The conductor looked at his feet and wondered where Marshall ran. The remaining guard had his gun drawn, but was extraordinarily shaky. The man walked toward the train from the right side slowly and took his first steps onto the train. The crowd of traders had now dispersed and were completely gone.

In the meantime, Marshall entered the conductor's car and saw the older waitress knocked out with a bloody lip. With his gun drawn, Marshall popped his head out from one of the windows on the left side of the conductor car. He stuck half of his body out so he could get a good shot but was still not visible to the conductor. The conductor was still scrambling and looking at his feet and surroundings. Marshall popped his body upward and shot the conductor twice in the chest, causing the conductor to fall backward toward his remaining goon.

Marshall then heard two shotgun shots and knew the back man had to reload. He quickly brought himself in from the window, ran toward the back of the conductor's car, and saw the man frozen with concern. Marshall saw the conductor lying dead on the train and saw bullet holes leading toward car two.

"Drop your weapon," yelled Marshall.

The man did what he was told and began whispering

"I didn't see her there...I swear I didn't mean it. I just got startled and fired," rambled the man.

Marshall held his gun on the man as he opened the door to see Ariel lying on her back in the middle of the car with shotgun wounds all through her torso and blood on her face. Marshall looked at the man with the door half open and fired three shots to the man's chest. The man fell backward off the train.

Marshall ran toward Ariel and grabbed her head, but already knew she had passed. Marshall's lip quivered with sadness. He looked up and saw all of the Soldiers in the previous cars taking a defensive position with their pistols. Marshall knew he would be remembered if they saw him any longer and would draw questions if he were not in West U.S. He turned around toward the conductor's car and saw the older waitress crying and walking toward him.

The waitress hugged him full of tears. "Thank you. Thank you so much. They've been abusing us for so long,"

The waitress still had not seen Ariel, because Marshall was standing in front of her body. The waitress let out a horrible scream as her eyes finally connected with the scene. She collapsed over Ariel's lifeless body.

"I'm sorry," Marshall said with a shaky voice, almost as if he was about to cry.

"You saved more than you know, young man. She can fly wherever she wants now," The waitress said hysterically crying over Ariel's body while staring at her.

"Do you know how to drive the train?"

"Yes, I do."

"Start the train now, and then you can grieve."

Marshall pulled the waitress away from Ariel and said, "I need this train to be moving."

"Of course, of course," The waitress said trying to recover from the tears and nodded her head.

The waitress walked toward the conductor's car and started the train. The train slowly started picking up speed. Marshall was in the bathroom staring at himself in the mirror knowing his decision was made for him. He locked the bathroom door behind him, grabbed both of his bags, and jumped out the window once the train began moving. He ran toward the forest line in hopes of concealing his identity.

Marshall turned around, once hidden in the trees, and saw the train drive away along with any chance of letting himself get close to another person again.

The last car seemed odd. He took a closer look before the train was out of sight. It looked as if there were three people on the car's roof.

CHAPTER 3

Whitehall *2040*

T wo miles south of Billings, Montana was the Fairbanks' family cabin. It was secluded by semi-dense woods on all sides with falling leaves surrounding the property. The wood cabin had two floors with no basement. There were three rooms on the second floor with one bathroom on this floor. On the main floor, there was a living room, kitchen, and one more bathroom.

Jerrod's father made the cabin. His father built the cabin to have a nice get-away from city life and to go hunting with his sons. The cabin served a more important purpose as time passed.

Jerrod's parents and many other families were part of a northern Madison Legacy Army Fort. Their mission was to defend the fort and the surrounding area. They were also watch-outs for any large military movements. Their fort was located near Whitehall, Montana.

The fort itself was simply as it was, four concrete walls protecting the habitants on the inside of the walls. Within the walls held six families with six houses and one watchtower. The families took shifts patrolling along the perimeter, staying alert to any possible threats.

Unfortunately, for the Whitehall base, one of the watch guards fell asleep on the job. There was a United States scout sniper sent to watch over the base and signaled the attack when the man in the tower fell asleep. Four helicopters from the United States flew over the U.S. soon-to-be finished walls and headed toward Whitehall, Montana.

The man in the tower awoke to the sight of four lights in the sky rushing toward their base. At this point, it was too late to stop the entirety of the attack, but the man did what he could. He rang the alarm to alert the rest of the fort members and grabbed a Stinger, an anti-air rocket launcher, and took aim at one of the choppers. The scout sniper finally received a clear shot and fired at the man striking him directly in the chest. The man fell limp and did not get up again.

The four choppers were given a go-ahead message and the choppers proceeded. The Soldiers of the Whitehall base scrambled for weapons while still saving as many as they could.

Jerrod was awoken by his father yelling, "You all need to get out of here!"

Jerrod, still half asleep, proceeded to do as he was told. His father ran outside firing his assault rifle into the sky. What followed was the sound of a missile being shot and striking the house next to Jerrod's. Jerrod's father stumbled into his house again and ran toward Jerrod who was holding his little brother, Tommy, in his arms.

"Take your brother and head to the cabin," said his father.

"Where's mom?"

"She's outside checking on everyone else. But you need to leave this second," exclaimed Jerrod's father.

Just as his father spoke, another explosion occurred. Jerrod sat there scared, thinking of how many of his family and friends were being attacked. Jerrod's father went to their gun safe in their house and handed Jerrod a hunting rifle and two pistols. He also handed Jerrod a bag of ammo, and then handed Tommy a bag of fruits.

"Take these and run, son. We'll be right behind you. Just go!"

Jerrod nodded his head, watched his father give his little brother a hug, and heard his father say, "You listen to everything Jerrod says."

His father looked at both of them and said, "I love you both so much, and I know your mother does, too. I'll see you both soon."

Jerrod looked at his father one last time, held his brother's hand, and ran out the back door. Jerrod's father ran out the front door to meet with his wife defending from the walls.

Jerrod dodged machine gun shots from above and then heard a missile hit. The explosion threw Tommy and Jerrod to the ground. They turned around and saw their home of the last few years had been destroyed.

Jerrod saw a girl from their camp named Natalie standing in fear and Jerrod yelled for her. Natalie turned and saw Jerrod waving to her.

Three buildings were now in flames, with debris and bullet-filled bodies throughout the base. A boy named Omar, who was the same age as Natalie and Jerrod, ran from behind and picked up Natalie. They ran toward Jerrod and Tommy, who were now on their feet. Together, they all ran for their underground shelter, which had an underground escape route leading them a half mile off base.

Jerrod opened the doors as the three of them ran down the stairs. Jerrod turned around, saw the mass of fire throughout his home, and saw four people shooting at the helicopters from the concrete wall, one was his mother. He heard a missile fire and saw the fire trail lead a path right toward his mother's position. Dust and debris were thrown into the air and complete silence entered Jerrod's head even with the amount of commotion surrounding him.

Another house blew up, and Jerrod stood watching and became emotionally unfazed at this point. Jerrod looked to his right and saw his grandfather shooting into the sky with his grandmother hugging him while crying. Jerrod felt the need to help even though he was told to leave. Jerrod ran toward his grandparents and began yelling.

"Come with me!" he said.

At first, his grandpa was hesitant but then Jerrod's grandma banged on the grandfather's chest. "He needs us more than you need this base," yelled the grandmother.

The grandfather looked down at his wife and nodded his head. All three of them ran toward the shelter, shutting and locking the door behind them to give them extra time should the United States Soldiers chose to follow.

Jerrod's father ran up to the watchtower, which was filled with bullet holes. The tower started to tilt. He looked at Omar's father who laid on the floor with lifeless eyes and a sniper shot to his chest. Jerrod's father grabbed the rocket launcher and aimed at a helicopter charging him with its machine gun firing.

Jerrod's father received the lock on needed to fire the weapon and did just that. The helicopter flying toward him burst into a fireball and crashed at the base of the tower. This caused the entire tower to collapse. Jerrod's father passed out after the collision.

★ ★ ★

He woke after a punch from a Soldier.

"How many people went through the tunnel last night?" yelled the Soldier as he punched the father in the face again.

"Fuck off!"

The Soldier interrogating Jerrod's father walked away to speak to the rest of his team. His father looked around to what was left of his fort in the daylight. Every building was burned to the ground, with smoke coming from all spots that used to hold houses. Each one of the four walls had a giant hole ensuring this base would never be used again. He saw a pile of bodies getting larger as

Soldiers threw more bodies onto the already burning mess. The father felt disgusted and started crying.

"Are you going to tell us how many people escaped? Or are you not?" asked the Soldier.

"I'm not," said the father while staring at the Soldier in his eyes.

"Fine." The Soldier grabbed his pistol from his side and shot the father in the head, killing him instantly. The body fell to the dirt, and the Soldier turned around to speak to the scout sniper.

"Sergeant Lawrence, I need you to go through the tunnel and track down anyone who escaped last night. We need to make sure no one spreads the word. Do you need a squad?"

"Just give me two of your Soldiers, and I'll be good. Too many people will be too nosy for this to work," said Sergeant Lawrence.

The three walked toward the tunnel, which was now opened and unlocked. On the other side of the tunnel, Jerrod and his grandpa waited for an ambush. The four others continued their walk toward the cabin. Jerrod was positioned fifty yards from the tunnel's opening. The opening of the tunnel was a hatch that opened upward. To get to the hatch, the person would need to climb a ladder. Jerrod was using a Winchester Model 70 for sniping, which was handed down to him from his grandfather. His grandfather, who was positioned twenty-five yards away from the opening of the hatch, had an M4 Carbine, which was mass-produced after the bombings. Both were ready to shoot at anyone who showed themselves.

Sergeant Lawrence and his Soldiers got to the end of the tunnel and found the ladder that led to the hatch.

"You climb to the top and toss a smoke grenade so we have cover when we get up there because I know they're watching. Run to the nearest cover you can find because they'll be shooting as soon as you're spotted," Sergeant Lawrence ordered.

Both Soldiers said, "Yes, Sir."

Both men rethought their decision to accept this mission. The Soldiers climbed the ladder, and threw the smoke grenade directly next to the top of the hatch.

Jerrod and Grandpa saw the smoke go off and both knew what was about to happen. They both aimed down their sights, knowing they would be popping up at any second. Sergeant Lawrence and his Soldiers waited for the smoke grenade to fully encapsulate the area so they had a greater chance of finding cover.

Once Sergeant Lawrence felt comfortable with sending in his troops, he did. The two climbed through the hatch, immersed in smoke. They slowly walked through it until they found cover. Sergeant Lawrence waited a second to hear gunfire but heard nothing and continued up the ladder and into the woods.

The hatch was positioned downhill from all surrounding land, with a few trees. Jerrod was crouched near a tree overlooking the now smoke-covered area. Grandpa was between two trees with his M4 peeking through the gap.

"There are too many open spots, Sir," exclaimed one of the Soldiers with nervousness running through his voice.

"Quiet down," said Lawrence angrily.

One of the Soldiers wandered too close to the edge of the smoke and Grandpa spotted him. Grandpa opened fire, spraying the Soldier and the surrounding area with bullets.

The Soldier shot first was hit with twelve bullets and flopped to the ground. Grandpa sprayed the rest of his magazine into the haze. Sergeant Lawrence managed to hide behind a tree on the opposite side of Grandpa. The other Soldier was hit twice in his right leg making him scream and collapse. The Soldier preceded to shoot blindly in Grandpa's direction but hit only dirt and trees. Grandpa ducked his head to reload and waited.

The smoke was beginning to clear, and Jerrod was positioned opposite his grandpa. He had a clear shot at Sergeant Lawrence. Sergeant Lawrence looked up to see the glare of sun in Jerrod's scope aiming directly at him.

"Dammit," whispered Lawrence before he heard a shot fired.

The shot hit Sergeant Lawrence in the upper right shoulder causing him to fall to the ground. Jerrod emptied the blank shell from his previous shot and saw Sergeant Lawrence running to the left. The smoke was now completely gone, and Jerrod saw his grandpa was under fire from a Soldier laying on his back because he was unable to stand.

Jerrod took aim at the Soldier shooting toward his grandpa, aiming for the dead center of his back. He pulled the trigger. The shot was a direct hit, and the man fell completely to his back dying almost instantly after being shot. Grandpa, hearing the shots had subsided, peeked around his tree and saw the two dead men lying on the ground. Grandpa also saw Sergeant Lawrence running away and watched as Jerrod followed his target with his scope.

Sergeant Lawrence collapsed behind a rotting tree that protected him from Jerrod's sight. Jerrod knew he needed to reposition. Sergeant Lawrence knew Jerrod's last position and would be searching there first.

During this time, Grandpa walked over to the two Soldiers lying dead on the grass and dirt. Grandpa fired a point blank shot to both of their heads to confirm their deaths. He grabbed a grenade from one of the men's tactical vests. Grandpa held his thumb to the grenade and pushed the top down, causing it to be a live grenade. After throwing it, there was a two-second delay. Grandpa tossed the grenade down the tunnel to destroy another attack that might be forming.

Hearing the boom, Jerrod looked back to see if Grandpa was fine and then continued to do his job. Grandpa ran up the hill to flank the enemy from a different direction.

Sergeant Lawrence knew the severity of his situation and planned an attack strategy. He had grenades of his own and started to throw them in Jerrod's last known position in hopes of getting a lucky kill. One grenade landed near Grandpa and knocked him to the ground, but he was uninjured. Lawrence took the scope off his rifle, peeked above the log protecting him. and searched for Jerrod.

Jerrod climbed to the top of a leafed tree, protecting himself from being seen. Lawrence panicked, as he could not see Jerrod, which Jerrod could see through his scope. Jerrod fired a shot from the tree, hitting Lawrence in his left shoulder, and knocking him backward to the ground.

Lawrence rolled around trying to get himself up but could not do it due to the pain from his wounds. Grandpa ran up to his position and kicked Lawrence in the face. Grandpa signaled to Jerrod everything was safe, and Jerrod moved toward Grandpa.

Grandpa grabbed all of Lawrence's weapons off his tactical vest and positioned him sitting up on the log that was once protecting him.

"You're going to bleed-out unless we help you, so give me some answers," said Grandpa in a calm tone.

"I don't rat on the U.S."

"You better start if you want to see the United States again," said Grandpa as he knelt down and got closer to Lawrence.

"How many of you are following us?"

Lawrence remained silent for a second but realized he was losing feeling in his right hand. Lawrence wanted to cooperate so he could receive medical help, but he still did not want to betray the United States. He decided to lie.

"There's no one else coming. No one will be looking for us," said Lawrence.

"Is there anyone from the fort still alive?"

"We torched everyone but you two," said Lawrence smugly, knowing his end was coming.

Grandpa turned to Jerrod and said, "You see that ear bud looking thing on his strap?"

"Yes," replied Jerrod.

"Well, that's a location device. His comrades will be heading to this point once they see it's not moving anymore. If we destroy it, they'll most definitely know something went wrong. So let's give the United States Army a welcome gift."

Grandpa looked back toward Lawrence who was starting to look paler and was gazing off into the distance.

"Now that you lied to me, we have no use for you, and we're not going to carry you all the way...," while speaking, Grandpa stood up and shot Lawrence in the face.

"Help me set up for the next attack," said Grandpa as he looked toward Jerrod with a new found respect of bravery.

"We're not going to be anywhere near here for the next attack. The cabin needs us more, and now we have a lot more weapons. Grab all of the grenades, weapons, and ammo from the Soldiers but first drag this one down to the others," said Jerrod's grandfather.

"Yes, Sir," said Jerrod who began to drag the body down the hill.

Two days later Jerrod and Grandpa approached the cabin. The two laid on the ground with their sniper rifles pointed toward the cabin to make sure there were no threats in the area. The two waited an hour watching for movement and then preceded to walk toward the cabin.

Tommy saw the two coming to the door and ran outside hugging them both.

"You guys made it," yelled Tommy with a smile and a sense of relief.

Omar, Natalie, and Jerrod's grandma all ran outside and formed a group hug.

Grandpa ended the reunion to give everyone the bad news.

"We're the last of Fort Whitehall... No one else made it out," said Grandpa as he began to cry along with everyone else in the group except for Omar and Jerrod.

Grandma slapped both of them and said, "You aren't looking any manlier for not crying."

As if on cue, the two broke down as Jerrod's grandma comforted them both while the whole family cried together.

Grandpa tried to rally himself to give one more speech. "We're all family now and we all have to look after each other. This is our new home, and we will defend it to the end. The U.S. shouldn't find us here. If they do, we'll take as many of them out as we can. I'm not only a grandpa to just Tommy and Jerrod; I'm a grandpa to you two, too."

Grandma said, "The same goes for me, too, kids. We are all family, and I will take care of you all until my last day."

"We can have our sorrow now, but I'm going to teach all of you to be top shots and Soldiers. We'll defend this cabin with the highest of skills. Your parents are proud of you for fighting, and they'll be with us through the rest of our journey here," said Grandpa in a reassuring voice.

"What if they send more helicopters?" cried Tommy.

"They wouldn't send helicopters too far away from their base. They don't want us recovering parts from a potentially downed helicopter. So, don't worry about that at all, Tommy. We'll be safe here and, if not, you'll be trained to make it safe."

The six hugged each other in front of the cabin knowing their entire world was in arm's distance.

★ ★ ★

At the tunnel's hatch, forty-eight hours had passed without receiving contact from Sergeant Lawrence or his troops. The General of United States Militia ordered a recon mission for the three men. He sent thirty troops down the tunnel to find them. The troops knew the general idea of where they could be because of the GPS.

The thirty troops reached the end of the tunnel and saw a Soldier hung from the top of the tunnel's hatch with blood dripping down his lifeless body. All thirty Soldiers stood in fear not knowing what they were up against anymore.

One Soldier was ordered forward to put the man's body on the ground. As he approached, it was revealed that the stomach area of the dead man's shirt was soaked in blood.

"Sir, the body is tied to the top of the hatch," said a Soldier.

"Well, cut down the poor bastard," said the Soldier in charge.

The Soldier did as he was told. More Soldiers walked toward the ladder. The Soldier who cut the man down was now trying to open the hatch but there was a heavy resistance. The Soldier continued to struggle until it popped open.

Once open, he saw the trip wire holding it shut had snapped. He heard something falling and looked toward the commotion. Sergeant Lawrence's body was hung from a tree directly above the hatch and his body fell onto the Soldier forcing him to fall down the hatch.

Meanwhile, the Soldier in charge cut open the shirt of the man hanging in the tunnel and found his stomach was cut out and replaced with seven grenades. He panicked as Lawrence's body fell down from the tree and into the tunnel. He saw Sergeant Lawrence also had an incendiary grenade in his mouth that was pulled. On impact, it fell out of his mouth.

The erupting fire spread through the tunnel causing the seven grenades to explode. All thirty Soldiers were killed.

Whitehall survivors were not considered a priority kill at this point and were not pursued further, due to the high risk factor with minimal benefit.

The war ended in 2044. The six Whitehall survivors continued to live in the cabin. The six were firm Madison Legacy supporters, but were too attached to the sentimental value of the cabin to move south to Madison's capital and safety.

CHAPTER 4

Déjà vu   *May 2, 2046*

It was not a normal morning for Jerrod, Omar, and Natalie. The now twenty-two-year-olds were finally given permission from their grandparents to head back to Whitehall to see their old home. Tommy was not allowed to go, because he was only fourteen.

All three were extremely nervous about what they would find and what the world was like away from the cabin. The Fairbanks family and friends were frequent visitors to the city of Billings, which was only two miles away from their home. There, they traded the animals they hunted with the other people in the area. The Fairbanks also had a small garden and a pond close to the cabin. This provided clean water once boiled down and also provided another trading tool with the city of Billings. The Fairbanks used the food and water to get ammo from Billings for hunting and target practice. The family was accustomed to this small area. It had been six years since any of them had headed west. However, today was the day.

Jerrod received a tip from a friend in Billings that the Eagle stopped to make trades just ten miles south of their location. Jerrod figured he could sneak onto the train and get a free ride to Whitehall. Jerrod shared this idea with his family, and his grandparents decided today was the greatest opportunity to leave for Whitehall.

The family knew they could have all walked or borrowed horses from Billings to Whitehall over the past years, but this would save time and money for the trip.

Jerrod, Natalie, and Omar were all well-armed and well-supplied for their journey. They hoped to find the bunker underneath the watchtower. Their grandpa told them there would be tons of supplies to gather in the bunker. Grandpa never felt the need to head back, but with recent sightings of people with guns in the area, he felt it was finally necessary to re-supply.

Jerrod was armed with his grandfather's sniper rifle. Omar was armed with an M12 Carbine and a pistol for each of them. Natalie was armed with a Remington 870 12-gauge, which was traded for last year. All three of these newly created Soldiers were ace shots due to the great teachings of their grandfather. Grandpa also taught everyone in the cabin to be tactical and smart when engaging an enemy.

Only on a few occasions did anyone in the cabin have to raise their weapon to another person. No one in the cabin had fired at someone since the attack on Whitehall. The family practiced shooting targets and had taken down hundreds of deer and small animals over the past six years. All members of the household were trained for the worst.

Grandma ran up to all three of them and gave a giant hug.

"You all better be so safe while you're gone," cried Grandma.

"You watch out for one another. Family is all we have, so you must protect each other."

Grandma began crying out of worry of what could go wrong on the trip. "Grandma, you know we'll be safe. Grandpa has taught us everything we should know about defending ourselves," said Jerrod.

"Believe me, there's a lot more I can teach you, son," said Grandpa, who was now standing with the group in the doorway.

"The three of you know enough now to be safe, but I will never run out of things to teach you kids." Grandpa leaned in for another group hug with the three of them. Tommy was in his room frustrated that his grandparents would not allow him to head out on this adventure.

"Make sure Tommy doesn't stay mad at us for long," laughed Jerrod.

"Do not worry, dear, he'll have fun with us while you're gone," said Grandma with reassurance.

The group gave their last goodbyes to each other before turning their backs and walking south. It was going to take a couple of hours to get to the train. This would work out perfectly, because it would be dark by then. This would give the team an element of extra stealth from the Soldiers aboard the train.

"Omar, you're already snacking?" asked Natalie with a laugh.

"Hey, I eat my food when I please, and you can eat yours as you please," said Omar.

"And we know you will," joked Jerrod who looked toward Natalie.

Natalie gave a grin toward Jerrod and then lightly hit him on the shoulder.

"You guys are just upset that my tiny self can outrun you two," joked Natalie.

"Oh, please, Natalie, you'll need a bike and a mile head start to outrun me," said Omar

The three of them continued to joke around as they walked deeper into the woods and closer to the Eagle. Jerrod let his hand rub against Natalie's. The two met eyes and they began holding hands.

Natalie and Jerrod had been dating for four years. With spending so much time together in the same house, feelings developed. Both of them knew what the other person had endured, and they were constantly there for each other. Natalie and Jerrod were inseparable.

Omar had a few relationships with women from Billings, but none of them lasted longer than a few months. Omar loved to joke around, which made it hard for women to find the serious side of him. Omar loved being the one to make a group laugh, but everyone in the house knew he was just as deadly as anyone else, despite his sense of humor.

Natalie had developed a kind personality over the years. She was very pleasant and talkative regardless of the trauma she experienced with the attack at Whitehall. She was the most competitive person in the house, and she would do whatever she could not to lose. She had been given the same combat train-ing as Omar and Jerrod and was equally capable of fighting. Natalie preferred her shotgun to the standard assault rifle due to the spread shot and quick hip fire.

Jerrod grew into a calm, quiet individual. Jerrod spoke when he felt it was needed or joked around with his family. Strangers, however, rarely heard Jerrod speak. Jerrod loved talking to Natalie. The two had a bond no one could break. The two would be together until something forced them apart. Over the years, Jerrod brought his sniping skills to unrealistic levels. Jerrod was an amazing sniper when he was younger and sniped with his father. Today, Jerrod was the world's greatest shot, but he remained modest.

Jerrod loved his little brother, Tommy, but Tommy had a darker personal-ity than the rest of the family. Tommy kept to himself whenever he could. Tommy had a dark look on the world and just never became happy again after the tragedy at Whitehall. Grandpa always hesitated to teach him how to use a weapon, because he did not know if he could trust Tommy. The family felt there was no fourteen-year-old boy in Tommy's body. They felt there was a bitter war veteran that could never accept their loss.

Jerrod, Natalie, and Omar finally made it to where the train was supposed to make its stop. They could already see a small group gathering with supplies to trade with the Soldiers on the train.

"Let's keep our distance from them. I haven't seen them in Billings before so let's not be too friendly just yet," said Jerrod with leadership echoing in his voice.

Omar and Natalie both understood Jerrod was the leader when Grandpa was not there. Jerrod was a natural leader and took the load of responsibility with no hesitation. Jerrod was raised by his father who was also a natural leader. Natalie may have been a competitive person, but she knew when something related to a life-or-death decision, Jerrod would take the responsibility.

The three set up some small metal pegs to be stabbed into trees to climb. The three of them climbed up a nearby tree that overlooked the railway, while still keeping an eye on the group of traders. The traders seemed non-hostile, but there was no need to take a chance.

Several hours passed and more groups of traders arrived. Jerrod recognized some citizens of Billings. The three of them decided to stay in the tree so there was no need to jump down yet. Eventually, there were around forty people waiting to exchange items with members of the Eagle.

"Natalie, I see the train. Wake up, Omar."

Jerrod had the safety on his rifle turned on while he followed the train with his scope. The train slowed to a complete stop. Jerrod looked through each of the windows in the train cars and saw a man in the front begin to stand. He seemed frustrated.

"Jerrod, the traders are moving up to the tree line," said Natalie.

Two men exited the front of the train with some boxes of supplies to trade. The traders brought all of their supplies past the tree line into the empty quarter mile of dirt that separated the train from the woods.

"What's the plans, boss?" asked Omar with a smile on his face. Jerrod hated it when they called him boss.

"They have a sniper on the top of the front car of the train. I have my scope on him and he doesn't seem to be paying attention to his surroundings. Omar, you head to the tree line directly across from the last train car. We'll hop on there when the last box is traded so they don't pay attention to us," Jerrod ordered.

Omar did as he was directed, slung his gun from his hands to his back, and descended from the tree. He scouted out the area and made it to a bush right on the edge of the tree line. Jerrod signaled to Omar he was clear from the sniper, and Omar signaled to Jerrod that he was safe.

"Natalie, I think something's about to happen," said Jerrod.

"What do you mean?"

"A man just stabbed one of the traders."

They heard screaming and arguing, and Omar looked to Jerrod to receive a signal on what was happening. Natalie signaled back they were still safe. Just after Natalie signaled, the group heard shots from a pistol.

"The sniper's down Natalie. Tell Omar."

"The traders are running back to the forest, so the train's probably leaving soon. Head to Omar, and I'll stay lookout for a little longer," said Jerrod

Natalie grabbed all of her supplies and Jerrod's. She headed toward the bush where Omar was stationed. Jerrod saw a man with pure rage in his eyes and his body was covered in blood. Jerrod could not see exactly what was happening but assumed someone innocent was injured or killed. Jerrod saw all of the traders run underneath him. Once it was clear, Jerrod jumped down and ran to Natalie and Omar who were both ready to run to the train.

The train slowly moved as the three of them saw a man walking away from the train.

"What's he doing?" questioned Omar.

"I don't know, and I don't wish to find out. Let's go," stated Jerrod.

The three of them ran to the train that was working up to full speed. Jerrod got on one knee and positioned his hand to help give Natalie and Omar a push for when they jumped to the top of the train. Once the two were up, Omar and Natalie reached out their hands to pull Jerrod to the roof of the car.

"Lay on your backs," said Jerrod.

Natalie and Omar did just that, and the three rode the train completely in stealth. Not one Soldier knew they were on top of the train except for Marshall, who was now miles behind them.

"Natalie, how long did you say we would be up here?" asked Jerrod.

"About an hour and half, and then we should hop off," she replied.

"Well, you two can take a quick nap if you want, because I napped last," said Omar.

Natalie fell right to sleep. Jerrod was unable to sleep and just stared up into the sky.

"Everything good, Jerrod?" asked Omar.

"Just a little tense."

"What for? The hard part is over, bud."

"I'm just out of my comfort zone. Anywhere outside of the cabin feels unsafe to me," Jerrod admitted.

"Even Billings?"

"Especially Billings. There are so many people in that city. The fact the cabin is so close to Billings worries me. Plus, why do you think that man got off the train?"

"I don't know," admitted Omar.

"He's a scout. Something bad is coming. Why else would those men on the train need to trade with scum like us in unclaimed lands? Something bad is happening in the States, so they are looking for land to move to again."

"How do you know all of this?" asked Omar.

"Grandpa told me about a lot of the wars he lived through, and I read in our history books about what happened to people who said 'no' to a higher power. They let us live in peace for this long, but that'll soon be ending. If they kill us, they basically kill any chance of Madison ever having a hold in the north."

"Why are we leaving the cabin if you're so afraid of what's coming to us?"

"Well, we're getting weapons and hopefully a vehicle to resupply us for this inevitable war. At that point, Grandpa's going to the mountains for one last training session. Then, we'll be ready. We'll be able to kill anyone that threatens us. I won't let any of us die because of the U.S. or whoever," said Jerrod. His voice cracked toward the end of the sentence signaling the stress and concern inside of his head.

Omar reached over and gave him a re-assuring grab on his shoulder.

"I love you, brother, and we're going to kill all of the stupid Statesmen. As long as we have family, we have everything we'll ever need," said Omar.

"A gun wouldn't hurt though," said Jerrod.

"Let's get these guns and head back home as soon as possible so we can be on our way to becoming bad-asses," said Omar with a confident smile on his face.

The train was getting closer to the drop off point. Jerrod woke Natalie and gave her a kiss on her cheek.

"Let's go, girl."

"You ready Omar?" asked Jerrod.

"You know I am!" yelled Omar, creating enthusiasm for all.

Natalie gave the signal to Jerrod and Omar that this was the location closest to Whitehall. All three were equipped with a miniature raft the family found years ago and finally had a reason to use the rafts. All of them jumped on the side of the raft and all landed safely. The three of them gathered their items and walked toward the tree line of this new location. They knew exactly where to go.

"We're about an hour's walk away from Whitehall if you two just want to rest for the remainder of the night? We can stay in one of these trees to be safe," said Natalie.

"That sounds good. We have a very long walk tomorrow back home, so let's eat and sleep in the tree. I will take first watch," said Jerrod.

The three of them climbed the tree and opened their canned foods. Omar and Natalie promptly fell asleep after their meals, but Jerrod remained awake watching the surrounding unknown area.

Hundreds of horrifying thoughts entered Jerrod's head of what could be happening at the cabin with half of the family not home to protect it. He worried for Tommy because Tommy could not be with them and wished Tommy would be happier in life. He worried about his grandparents since they were getting older and less capable of defending themselves. Jerrod remained awake the entire night having thoughts of worry enter his mind.

Natalie woke up to the sight of Jerrod staring off into space with red-strained eyes.

"Babe, you didn't wake either of us up to trade shifts!"

"I couldn't sleep Nat," Jerrod replied.

Natalie moved closer to Jerrod and gave him a hug.

"What's wrong?"

"I'm worried about us and everyone still back at the cabin."

"Well, you can't worry about something we have no control over. We can't protect our grandparents and Tommy right now, so you shouldn't carry that weight, Jerrod."

"I know you're right, I just can't escape this thought."

"Well, we can move out now so we can get home to the cabin sooner, Jerrod. That'll relieve some of your tension," said Natalie.

Natalie woke up Omar, and all three of them began their final stretch to Whitehall. Jerrod figured there would be squatters living in or around the ruins. With this in mind, all members of the team remained silent and ready to fire. Beyond their last hill, a small cabin was situated in front of them.

Jerrod, Omar, and Natalie immediately dropped to the ground and waited for Jerrod's command. Jerrod had his lens sighted on the front door of the cabin. The group remained still and silent for a half an hour but still saw no movement.

"Natalie, I need you to clear this house. Omar follow behind her. I'll stay over-watch."

"You got it," said Natalie.

Natalie and Omar went into a crouch position and slowly moved forward. Natalie had her shotgun ready to fire and approached the front door. The door itself was open just a crack. She signaled to Omar to kick the door in, and Natalie would rush into the cabin.

Omar was given the nod by Natalie that she was ready to move. Natalie then noticed a trip wire attached to the door and tackled Omar who was in kick position. Both fell to the floor.

"What're you doing?" whispered Omar.

"There's a bomb inside there, I saw the trip wire."

Natalie signaled to Jerrod it was all clear and Jerrod ran toward the cabin.

"What happened?"

"There's a trip wire in there, Jerrod," said Natalie.

"I guess whoever lives here didn't want any intruders," said Omar.

"That, or whoever cleared this house wanted to kill anyone who wasn't here for the raid," said Jerrod.

"We should keep moving to the base. If any explosions happen, there could be a team around here and will be ready to clear the area," said Jerrod.

Natalie and Omar knew to agree with Jerrod on these subjects and both nodded. The three of them walked up the last hill that led to the grass plain where the fort was. All stood on top of the hill looking at the remains of their old home. A wave of memories and sadness hit each of them. They knew they were finally getting a sense of closure for what happened to their families.

Jerrod scoped out the area and saw absolutely no one near Whitehall. He figured this was because of how close this area was to the U.S. walls. Anyone living in this area was exterminated during the war and anyone who moved in was sure to be killed by the new attacks that Jerrod believed were occurring.

"All right, let's make this trip fast and efficient. We find the weapons and look for a vehicle to get us home faster, and then we're out of here. We're closer to the U.S. wall than I'd like to be."

The three of them descended down the hill and into the grass valley. They saw the spot where the opening gate used to stand. The three were reminded of the first day they moved here. This time the gate did not need to be opened, as it was completely gone. All four walls protecting the outpost had a large piece missing in the center. The fort was completely useless as a form of defense. All of the wooden barracks the families were raised in were burned to the ground and complete rubble. The tower that stood as the fortresses' eye laid flat on the ground, bent at the base.

"This is where Grandpa said to look," said Jerrod as he moved the debris to get to a hidden latch.

Jerrod and Omar moved all of the debris as Natalie stayed lookout to make sure they were not falling into a trap.

"I think this is it," yelled Omar.

It was a simple concrete base, but a few solid hits to a specific spot resulted in the cement seal popping open. Jerrod did just that as he took a metal rod and struck the cement, listening for the spot, which had a different pitch. Jerrod found the spot and struck it four times.

On the fourth try, the cement collapsed down a short tunnel. This revealed a ladder, which lead to a basement. Jerrod and Omar climbed down the tunnel to see where it lead. To their surprise and luck, it was exactly as described by their grandfather. It was a long tunnel that was only six feet tall and held gun racks filled with weapons and ammo boxes. There were also dozens of boxes filled with canned foods and bottled water. Jerrod and Omar looked at each other and knew they had hit the jackpot of supplies. The two shouted to Natalie that they found the weapons.

Jerrod and Omar grabbed bags to fill with ammo and food. They also grabbed a couple less-used versions of their own weapons. They could not carry all of the weapons so they left most of the weapons on the racks. They filled as many bags as they could with ammo and food and realized they could not carry all of this weight.

Jerrod sat with all of the bags contemplating on how to handle this situation. He then saw Omar hitting the back wall to this shelter.

"I think there's another hidden shelter," yelled Omar in excitement.

The wall collapsed as Omar hit the cement with the butt of a gun. Omar saw the room open up to a truck facing the other direction.

"Now how the fuck are we going to get this out of here?" asked Omar.

Jerrod looked around the room and saw a switch. Jerrod looked around to see if there was any chance this could be a trap. Jerrod felt safe and proceeded to push the button. Sunlight appeared where darkness used to be at the bottom of the wall. The button operated a door that lifted open. The door was buried underneath a few feet of dirt so it would not be found. The garage door was powered by sunlight as most of household utilities were nowadays. Vehicles still seem to be heavily reliant on gas, so many of the solar powered cars only belonged within the U.S.

Jerrod and Omar looked to each other with giant grins on their faces and both ran to get Natalie. The three loaded the bags into the truck's bed. They were able to fit everything and also had room for some canisters of gasoline.

"Hey has anyone here actually driven before?" asked Omar.

The group looked at each other, knowing none of them had driven a vehicle.

"Let's just take it very slow to begin with and we'll eventually get the hang of it," joked Jerrod trying to rationalize the situation.

Jerrod, Omar, and Natalie were ready to begin their trip east back home to the cabin full of ammo, weapons, food, water, and a new vehicle.

Jerrod walked over to the fort from the truck and stood remembering all of the good times he had with his parents and began to speak.

"I love you, Mom and Dad. I miss you and think about you every day. I'm taking care of the house like you wanted me to do, and I'm doing my best to make sure Tommy is happy. Which isn't the easiest might I add. You'd be proud of the Soldier I've become and the Soldiers Natalie and Omar have become. I don't know if I will ever come back to this fort. If that's the case, I would just like to say goodbye one last time. You taught me everything about being an honorable person in society, and I can only hope I'm making you proud in that respect. Rest in peace, Mom and Dad, and someday we'll catch up."

He knew his father was proud of him, and it felt good to be this close to his childhood home. Jerrod, Natalie, and Omar had accepted the pain that was dealt that day and were all confident their parents are looking upon them with pride.

"It was sad coming back, but this was the closure we all needed and the supplies we needed," said Natalie sounding as if she was trying to convince herself everything was okay.

Natalie teared up and Jerrod put his arm around her, as Omar was driving off road heading east back to their home.

"We all have each other, Natalie, and we'll see our parents someday. But for now, let's make the most out of every day," said Jerrod, trying to give a pep talk to the team as they drove away from Whitehall.

CHAPTER 5

Clearing Team   *May 2, 2046*

arshall had been walking for an hour looking for his team, which should be closing in on him. He had his gear in his bags and was ready to begin the next phase of this plan. Marshall was unable to think clearly with Ariel in the back of his mind. An ambush on Marshall was more likely due to his lack of awareness with his mind preoccupied.

Darkness engulfed the area with only minimal visibility with plain sight. Marshall put his night vision goggles on and continued heading north looking for the rendezvous point. Marshall was getting his head back in the mission and remembered he was here to train for the soon-to-be war. He remembered he fights for his mother and he would avenge her.

Marshall thought again how the United States killed another girl he admired. No matter what side he chooses, someone would want to hurt him and his family. Marshall was constantly being torn away from the idea the United States was a perfect place.

Mid-thought Marshall saw a man in a tree. Marshall immediately dropped to the ground and readied his sniper rifle toward the tree. It was extraordinarily dark with the trees hiding the moonlight. The sniper in the tree was not facing him, so he crawled forward to see if he could see where the sniper was aiming. What he saw was a cabin with a light on in the house and four men playing cards together.

Marshall kept an eye on the sniper in the tree but was also focusing his scope on the four men in the cabin. All four looked old enough to fight, and Marshall saw a hunting rifle directly next to the table. A light from eighty feet away began flashing. Marshall immediately knew he met up with the Elitists. The sniper in the tree was part of the team. A man in full black moved toward Marshall. The man laid down right next to him.

"You Marshall?" asked the Soldier.

"Yes, Sir."

"Well, you missed your jump-off point didn't you, boy?"

"Sorry, Sir, there was an altercation on the train."

"That's all right, if it wasn't for you, we would have missed this cabin. By the way, you can call me Eros."

"Like the god, Sir?"

"In the flesh, Soldier. We'll give you a nickname over time. So, just call me Eros from now on. I would introduce you to the rest of the team, but they're currently in position."

"Could you give me some background on this cabin, Eros?"

"Oh yeah, of course. Well, I don't know how much information was given to you within the walls, but some Madisons have been setting up in the north. Our job is to eliminate them."

"I was told I would be training in Billings," said Marshall.

"You will be. You and I will be heading to Billings bright and early tomorrow. But tonight we may as well help the U.S. cause, am I right? In front of us is an outpost cabin for trade between Madison and its cabins up north. There are dozens of these cabins surrounding Billings. Our current mission is to exterminate them. As you can see, there are four men playing poker, but what you missed is there are two more men patrolling that way and two more men patrolling the other way. The shift change is happening soon I'm guessing,"

"Are they threats to the U.S.?"

"Are you shitting me, Soldier? Just because their gun isn't pointed at you right this second doesn't mean they're friendlies. It's our belief the Canadians are teaming up with Madisons. This is why we think another war is coming. But I recruited a fine sniper like you to kill these men with minimal risk to the team."

Two men both west and east of the cabin appeared and walked toward the cabin. Marshall was looking through his scope and saw the men at the table look at their watches knowing their shift change was nearing.

"Right on time. Now if you'll excuse me, we'll continue this conversation in about three minutes. Please stay here. You'll lead the next assault, so don't worry my friend, you'll get some blood on your hands," said Eros casually.

Marshall did as he was told and stayed put while Eros ran east to hide behind a tree. The four men now all met in the center and four more men walked out of the cabin. The group exchanged friendly conversations and Marshall could see smiles on their faces. The four men went into the cabin and turned off the lights. Two men headed east on the same path from which the others emerged, while the other two men headed west.

Simultaneously, the two men heading east were killed by Eros and another man. Just as the two walked past a tree, Eros shot one man in the neck, while the other man had his knee sliced open with a large knife causing the man to drop while the knife slit his throat on the back swing.

"Hey, noobie, watch this," said a voice from the tree.

Marshall looked west and saw a man get sniped in the head, immediately causing him to drop. At the same time that happened, a womanly figure appeared and shot the other man in the head. This team killed four Madisons in a matter of seconds. Marshall looked back toward the cabin with his sniper rifle and saw a large muscular shadow of an Elitist enter the cabin. No noise was heard, but after thirty seconds, the muscular man came out of the cabin with a thumbs-up.

The sniper hopped down from the tree and walked toward the cabin. Marshall was still shocked with the ease this team had executing eight men. Marshall had always been a good shot but had never been a part of a stealth team. Marshall was used to having his enemy know bullets were coming. He felt more honor in that but could also see the safety and ease of killing an enemy that had no idea a team even existed. Marshall was beginning to piece together his role in the next war.

Eros signaled over to Marshall. Marshall gathered his belongings and headed to the cabin.

"Well, Marshall, here's your new team," said Eros with excitement. The five members of the Elitists and Marshall stood in a circle all facing each other.

"We have Ares, Tartarus, better known as Tar, Nyx, Themis, and myself. We are the Elitists, and we're your new team. You have a deadly set of skills, and I picked you out of thousands of other Soldiers. I think you'll be the greatest help to this team because you also have a motherly motive to kill these inbreeds," said Eros with a smile on his face.

Marshall was frustrated with Eros, with his calm and joyful presence even after talking about murder and the tragic death of his mother. Eros saw the frustration on Marshall's face but did not care enough to acknowledge the situation.

"I'm sure we'll all be best friends by the end of the night but why don't you help the team move these bodies to inside the building," said Eros.

Marshall obeyed his orders. He grabbed a body and started moving it toward the cabin. Ares was moving the other body next to him. Ares was the sniper in the tree.

"Hey, we know each other don't we?" asked Ares.

"Yeah, I think we graduated from the same sniper school," said Marshall.

"I hope you're still a good shot, because you're going to need some major skill to keep up with me. I'm the greatest sniper in the States, and I'm not going to let your new ass trump me. You got it?" Ares bragged.

In most circumstances, Marshall would not tolerate this level of intimidation, but Marshall was in an unknown environment with five other people who just showed off their killing masteries. Marshall looked toward Ares.

"I'm here to do whatever Eros asks of me, so don't worry. I won't get in your way," said Marshall.

"You're damn right," laughed Ares.

Ares and Marshall dragged the bodies to the door and saw Tar untangling a trip wire.

"What are you doing there?" asked Marshall.

"I'm the explosives expert for the team, so I'm setting up a trip wire for the front door of this cabin. These cabins usually have monthly shifts, so the next shift that opens that door will be blasted away with my brilliance," said Tar.

"Got to love a man that loves his job. Am I right, Marshall?" asked Eros.

After his perimeter check, Eros walked toward the cabin where Ares and Marshall stood. Marshall was distraught with the level of tolerance while speaking about murder and death. Marshall was beyond comfortable with killing someone but that aspect did not lead a conversation so causally.

Marshall looked toward Nyx and Themis, who were pulling the bodies from the west.

"So what are your two specialties?" asked Marshall.

"We do the grunt work for the team and are the front-line killers. We ain't afraid of anyone," said Nyx.

Nyx was the only female of the group, but she could hold her own. It did not seem to Marshall that anyone even acknowledged the fact she was a woman. She was fantastic at stealth and brute force killing and that was what was needed to be accepted in this team.

Themis seemed like the stupid giant to Marshall. He looked like he could uproot a tree with his bare hands but failed to have the basics of communicating with another human. Themis was the same as Nyx, he killed for the team, and no one could be mad when the job was done.

The team threw the last body into the pile of bodies in the cabin. The stench was horrid and blood spilled all over the floor. The cold lifeless bodies now haunted the tiny cabin. Standing closest to the bodies was Eros. Eros pointed his finger at Marshall.

"Do you like breakfast food, Marshall?"

"What do you mean?" asked Marshall with pure confusion in his eyes and tone.

"What do you mean, what do I mean? It's a simply question,"

"Yes, I do Eros."

"Perfect, I know the perfect spot for tomorrow morning. I need to fill you in on the extent of this mission and the role you'll be playing for this team."

"The bomb is ready to be set Eros," yelled Tar from the doorframe.

"I guess it's time to never see this cabin again team," said Eros.

The Elitists walked out one-by-one and headed north. Tar was the last one to leave because he armed the trip wire to the bomb. If the door opened more than an inch or two, the entire front of the building would explode, causing death plus a great deal of debris.

"All right Marshall, we have a small underground bunker very close to Billings, and that's where we stay. We have a room for you there, and that's where you can unload all of your stuff. That will be your new home for the next few months while we train you for the inevitable war to come," said Eros in a semi-inspirational tone.

The team walked in a straight line with everyone seemingly on edge except for Eros. Marshall was getting strange vibes from Eros. He seemed way too happy for his job field. Every single member of this team seemed off-putting to Marshall. A team of killers should not act this way thought Marshall. Marshall had no idea what Eros meant about breakfast, and it gave Marshall even more anxiety than he already felt.

The team walked on untouched grass as they walked through the dark woods. There were too many trees to count, providing the perfect camouflage and visual protection from enemies. The team was dressed in all black, so it was hard for anyone to notice the team, let alone Marshall who had to keep up with everyone. Tar was walking behind Marshall. Marshall had a stressed and worried expression on his face. Tar moved in closer to Marshall to see how he was doing with the new environment and new team.

"Hey, Marshall, you good, Soldier?" asked Tar.

"Yeah, I'm good, just unsure where we're heading, so I'm on edge."

"That's what your profile check said. You're a very stressed person and that makes a good Soldier, my friend."

"All of you guys did a profile check on me?"

"No, Eros just shared the information with all of us. We need to know who we'll be sleeping next to over the coming months."

"How'd you get recruited for this job? I mean I should know who I'm sleeping next to over the next few months, too," asked Marshall.

Tar laughed a little and began explaining his story to Marshall.

"Well let's see…A few years back, I was enlisted in the army and my wife was diagnosed with brain cancer. I couldn't afford to remove the cancer on my Soldier's salary. Luckily, I'm a talented explosive technician and my skills were noticed. Did you know I can set a trip wire trap faster than any other person in the army?"

"I did not," admitted Marshall.

"Well, Eros found that out and needed someone for this team. I received a letter to meet with the General, which I'm sure you did, too. He did the background check on me and offered me an opportunity I couldn't say no to. He said he would pay for the cancer treatment procedure if I devoted the rest of my service to the Elitists. With that I said goodbye to my wife and headed out on the Eagle. I've been out here for a little less than a year now."

"Have you spoke to your wife since?" asked Marshall.

"No, I haven't heard anything, so I just need to trust their word and hope I get to see her when my service is done."

"Well, that's very admirable of you, and I wish the best to your wife."

"Thank you, Marshall. I hope by now she's been cancer-free for some time."

Marshall saw the hope and sadness Tar portrayed through his expressions. Marshall knew the pain and sadness of losing someone you love. Marshall did not understand the hope that Tar possessed though. Marshall never lived in mystery of a life or death situation for his loved ones. Marshall realized how hard it would be not knowing whether the person you love was still living. This reaffirmed his belief in the idea of never loving would be less traumatic than loving and losing.

Marshall moved past the emotions and wanted to know more about the other members of this squad.

"What's everyone else's story, Tar? We have time before we get to the camp right?" asked Marshall.

"Yeah, we got another hour or so of walking. I guess Ares is the easiest story, so I'll just tell you his first. He was a competitive warrior. He fought because that was what he was good at. He seemed to love beating another man on the field. It's kind of gross, in my opinion, to know someone who just loved to hurt people. But you saw Eros, so you know those two are a perfect pair. That's why Ares was recruited. I only kill when asked to, and I find no joy in doing so. I kill so my wife can live. Ares kills for a confidence boost and the thrill of winning."

"Why do we have murderers leading the offense in the upcoming war?" asked Marshall.

"Because they are the best at what they do. They stealthily kill enemies and eliminate potential threats. What better people to have doing this than someone without a conscious?" stated Tar in a defeated tone.

Marshall and Tar were out of listening distance from the rest of the group who were further ahead. The two continued to speak about the rest of the group as they walked through the dark woods to Marshall's new home.

"What about Themis and Nyx? The two seem to be inseparable since I met with the group," stated Marshall.

"The two of them balance each other so that's why they're close. Themis is obviously a scary man to fight with his size, but he will almost never say a word. The man just will not speak for whatever reason. He's kind of a big dummy. A scary, strong, and deadly dummy, but a dummy. He was recruited by Eros after he saw Themis pull the jaw off the man Themis was boxing. It was a death match at a base to keep the morale high among the Soldiers. Themis wanted to intimidate the next person he was going to fight, so he knocked his opponent out, broke his jaw with a couple more punches, reached into his mouth, and ripped the jaw out. Eros was watching the fight and must have enjoyed it. Themis became an Elitist the next day."

"We're living with a bunch of murders, aren't we?"

"Yes. We're on the winning team though, so let's keep it that way. We were both chosen for a reason, too, and if you're not doing this for someone, maybe you just get a thrill for killing, too…"

"Sorry to disappoint your prediction, but I just feel obliged to protect my nation. If My nation wants me to fight with these monsters, then that's what I'll do," stated Marshall.

"Well, I applaud you."

"What's Nyx's story?" asked Marshall.

"She's actually Themis's sister and her connection with Themis is how she got the job. Themis would not travel unless his sister accompanied him. Eros needed Themis so he asked Nyx to prove herself and then she joined the team. Themis is a brute force killer, whereas Nyx is a dirty killer. Eros needed proof she was worthy of being an Elitist so he set up a death match again. Nyx, being a semi-small woman, was placed against a six-foot muscle man. The man rushed Nyx in the ring. As the man cocked his fist back to swing, Nyx leaned forward, bit his throat, and slashed it open with her teeth. The man fell backward as Nyx continued to bite his throat until the man stopped moving. Eros's team began to assemble with strength and skill unseen by any Madison."

Just as Tar finished telling the story of Nyx, the two caught up with the rest of the team at the front of the underground bunker entrance. The entrance was a large tree that had been hollowed-out and completely gutted. The front of the tree was pulled open to reveal a hatch.

"I hope you won't be this slow all of the time Marshall. I know you were on a date with Tar, but you have to wake up early tomorrow to get some food with me," said Eros.

"Sorry, Sir, it won't happen again," said Marshall.

"Very good. Now let me show you to your room, and we all can get some sleep for the night."

Eros opened the hatch with a hand-scanner. The hand-scanner accepted his prints, and Eros spun the hatch top open.

"Ladies first," joked Eros as he pointed to Marshall. Eros laughed much harder than needed for this joke.

Marshall was not offended with the joke but worried about what kind of man was leading this team. Marshall climbed down the ladder to see a white room with a large table in the center and six closed doors. There were two doors on each of the three walls he was facing. Eros came down the ladder next.

"Well, there's your room right on the right, my friend. You'll be neighbors with Ares. He is in the room one over. So, if you ever need sugar, you'll be heading there. Put your stuff away and be geared up by seven. You and I will head to Billings, and you can see your training ground for the first time."

Marshall did just that and opened the door to a small room, which had a twin bed and a closet. Unlike the living room, which was white, the bedrooms where bleak, with shades of brown. Nothing else was in the room, so Marshall placed his items in the closet and laid on the bed. He felt no need to set an alarm, because he knew he would have trouble sleeping tonight and would be up early.

Just as Marshall got up to shut the bedroom door, Tar walked past, gave Marshall a nod, and continued on his way to his room. Marshall felt he could trust Tar, and Tar probably felt safe to have someone in the bunker who did not kill for fun.

Marshall returned to his bed and stared at his ceiling waiting for breakfast.

CHAPTER 6

Breakfast at Tina's   *May 3, 2046*

Marshall slept for a few hours during the night but was now getting ready for his outing with Eros. Marshall was feeling nervous to spend time with Eros, as he seemed to be completely different from any other leader Marshall had met. Eros came off untouched and unaffected by killing those men last night. If anything, Eros seemed to enjoy murdering and that was why Marshall was worried. What was to come with joining this team?

Eros opened the door to Marshall's bedroom.

"Oh, great. You're already ready. Let's get a move on it. If they've ran out of bacon, then it's your head," said Eros with a joking tone. Marshall was finding it harder and harder to determine when Eros was joking and when Eros was serious.

The two gathered their weapons and headed up the hatch.

"Ahh, I love the smell of morning air, don't you?" asked Eros.

"Yeah, it's very refreshing, Sir."

"You're damn right it is. You're going to have to learn to appreciate the simple things in life around here, because you'll need to be mentally on duty at all times over the next months."

"I understand, Sir, and I will do everything I can to be prepared for the missions you give me."

"I knew you were the right choice, Marshall," said Eros as he jokingly cried and then broke out with laughter.

"Well, we have some time to talk while we walk to Billings so let me fill you in on what our main purpose is. Last night, you saw my team kill some inbreeds who were positioned to report any odd activity. We are the odd activity. Our mission is to kill everyone at the dozens of outposts reporting to Madison and Canada. We're to intercept any messenger and kill them. With the killings in the Outliers, Madison cannot say for certain that the U.S. is the one doing the killings. It's a win-win for us. We get to weaken the Madison Legacy and any Canadians who feel the need to interfere without ever being blamed."

"It seems like you have a successful system. So why'd you want to recruit me?" asked Marshall.

"A sniper can only kill so many people at one time, so why not just recruit another? It's very simple why I wanted you. You're good at killing and being sneaky and those are the exact job requirements. To top it off, these inbreeds killed your mother, so I know you feel no guilt when you kill an enemy. Your mom burned to death in a train, and you couldn't save her. But you can kill those bombers' children with my team and feel some justice there." Eros smiled toward the end of his speech.

Marshall felt the need to punch Eros in the face for speaking of his mother but knew he could not assault a superior so he walked ahead in silence.

"I know you don't like it when I speak of your mother, but I need you to continue to know why you are fighting for me. Or should I say why you're fighting for your mom."

Eros and Marshall were now approaching the city of Billings. The two looked over the city and to Marshall's surprise, he saw people living there. Eros continued walking to the city as Marshall hesitantly followed but began to speak his mind.

"I thought this was a training ground, Eros."

"Oh, it is. There's just lots of moving targets, my friend," laughed Eros.

"None of these people are armed, and there are lots of kids just walking around," noted Marshall.

"I'm not going to shoot anyone right now, Marshall, so just relax. Billings is a booming city in the Outliers. There are actually several cities still surviving in the Outliers. But citizens within the walls must not know there's another choice to live and fight for the States," stated Eros.

"Are all of these people Madisons?" asked Marshall.

"Kind of. Some are Madisons, some are Canadians trading with the city, and some are just families who didn't want to move in with either of the reigning capitals. They even have horses out here to carry wagons full of supplies between Billings and Canada. But I don't want you to view them like that. I want you to view them all as enemies to the States. All have disobeyed the United States' orders, and all are traitors to our nation."

The city had four main streets with houses on the outside of the perimeter of the neighborhood. There were three buildings in the center of Billings that were about six stories tall. There were small restaurants and small general stores. It was a well-functioning city outside the walls of an organized civilization.

The two of them reached the city and walked through the streets passing by people.

"Should we be walking with our guns showing like this?" Marshall questioned.

"Stop worrying. Soldiers from Madison and Canada are entering and exiting this city all the time. The citizens here think nothing of us, and that's the way I love it. There's a little bit of a thrill, walking next to someone who you'll probably kill in a fight within the next few weeks. Do you feel it, too?" asked Eros.

Marshall did not respond but walked with a guilty look on his face and continued to worry he could be attacked by anyone at any second.

"You still look worried. Why don't we just get some breakfast at this place called Tina's? I'll then answer any question you have, and you can start focusing on this mission at hand."

Eros led Marshall to a small diner, where they were greeted by a younger woman who was the hostess.

"Just two today?" asked the hostess.

"Yep, just me and my friend today," answered Eros as he creepily smiled at the woman.

The hostess led Eros and Marshall to their table, and Marshall still looked horribly nervous.

The restaurant was filled with people not even second-looking Marshall and Eros. Seeing a few Soldiers with guns was a normal occurrence to the people of Billings. The hostess sat them at their table.

"Your waitress will be right over for you guys," she said with a smile.

"So what're you in the mood for?" asked Eros as he stared at the menu.

Marshall still looked surprised and continued to look guilty. Marshall had yet to look at the menu, when Eros chucked the menu at him with a pissed-off look on his face.

"Are you not a professional? Are you abandoning your mission, Soldier? I hired you for stealth and discretion, so please give me at least one of those!"

Marshall looked angrily toward Eros as he picked up the menu and started reading. He saw so many different options for what he could eat and was surprised at an organized civilization beyond the U.S. walls.

"I'm going to get the Paul Bunyan breakfast, Marshall. What's looking good for you?" asked Eros.

"I think I'm just going to get eggs and toast."

"That's it, Marshall? Breakfast is on me, and you're in the middle of the pig exchange with Canada, and you didn't get anything with pork?" Eros yelled to Marshall in a joking tone.

"I'll be fine with just eggs and toast, Sir."

"Whatever you say, Soldier. You're the one who's eating the stuff."

The waitress walked toward the pair, Marshall took a quick glimpse, and looked away not to stare because he still felt nervous. Marshall did not want any extra attention. He took a quick glance at Eros and noticed he was staring down the waitress as she walked our way, creating a light tension in the air.

"Hello, fellas. My name's Julie and I'll be your waitress this morning. What can I get for you two?"

"Hmm. Well, since you yourself are not a choice on the menu, I guess I'll have to just stick with Paul Bunyan," said Eros with a creepy smile on his face and a chuckle making himself laugh at his forwardness.

Marshall just stared at Eros and was shocked the waitress laughed. Marshall had nothing to say but felt the awkwardness and tension being created.

Julie looked to be around twenty-five years old, and Marshall could tell Eros was beyond infatuated with her.

"Well, aren't you cute, darling," said Julie with a flirtatious smile.

Eros stood up, put his arm around Julie, and whispered something to her. She smiled and the two of them both walked to the men's bathroom. As they were walking away, Eros turned around and told Marshall. "It'll be like five minutes, tops. I'll tell her you want the eggs and toast, so don't worry."

Marshall was dumbfounded with the level of unprofessionalism being displayed. Marshall thought to himself, Eros was speaking of killing everyone in the town, and now he was off having sex with one of the locals. Marshall looked around and inspected the area. He noticed not one person noticed him. No one cared he had an assault rifle. The restaurant had only about fifteen tables and all were filled with people.

Eros walked out of the bathroom with a smile on his face as he approached the table where they had been sitting together.

"Breakfast is coming, buddy, but just not as fast as me!" Eros laughed at his own joke. Marshall gave a small grin even though he did not find the joke funny.

"All right, so now that's out of the way, please tell me about any questions you have running through your head right now," Eros stated in a more serious tone as things started to become more professional.

"How did this place survive the war?" asked Marshall

"There are dozens of semi-big cities still around right now that were just not a priority for the military at the time of the war. We would have spread our troops too thin if we attacked every single small city across the Outliers. That's why you and I are here now. There's a war coming, and we're not going to let the Madisons hide away this time. We're destroying any places that could harbor enemies."

"How many cities have you conquered?"

"City-wise not too many, but my team has killed hundreds of people populating small cabin outposts throughout the Outliers. Having Tar on the team has been our saving grace because he can take out a large number of people all at once," said Eros boasting in confidence.

"Why don't you go check the bathroom stall closest to the wall in the men's bathroom? Once you're in there move one of the ceiling tiles and let me know what you see"

"Why don't you just tell me?" asked Marshall.

"Where's the theatre in that kind of reveal?" asked Eros jokingly.

Marshall was well aware Eros was not going to tell him. Marshall left his chair and walked toward the bathroom. Marshall accidently shouldered a man walking past him, and the man apologized. Marshall gave a friendly smile and continued walking. Killing while hidden was his skill; hiding in plain sight was a skill Marshall still needed to perfect.

Marshall reached the bathroom and to his surprise, everything was clean and shining. The walls, sinks, and toilets were all clean. He walked toward the last stall and shut the stall door behind him. Marshall looked toward the ceiling and saw the tile. He moved the tile and saw a round black item that Marshall could not properly recognize.

At that moment, Marshall realized it was a bomb hidden away at this small time restaurant. He put the ceiling tile back, left the stall, and headed back to the table with a distressed look on his face.

"I hope you washed your hands," said Eros as Marshall approached the table.

The food had arrived at the table, and Julie was walking away by the time Marshall sat.

"You're going to kill all of these people?" whispered Marshall.

"Eventually. Actually, hopefully these people will be dead within the next month," said Eros with no hint of whispering.

"You just saw one of the bombs Tar secretly placed throughout the city. Did you see the tallest tower in the center of town? That's an overnight hotel that will be filled with those bombs," stated Eros

Eros put his fork down from eating, leaned into Marshall, and started to whisper.

"This is the mission, Marshall. We're here to kill Madisons. Armed or non-armed is not my issue. Our boss is paying us large amounts of money to kill anyone that could be a potential threat. Having a finger that can pull a trigger makes all of these inbreeds a threat and that's why we need to kill everyone in this town. I hope you can understand this, Marshall."

Marshall just stared off into space trying to put together the fact he signed up for this. Eros spoke again realizing he was scaring Marshall for what was in store for him.

"What do you want to get out of your life, Marshall?"

Marshall did not have much to say at this moment and started to think what he wanted. Up until the train ride, Marshall wanted to be the greatest war hero the United States had ever seen. Now Marshall began to realize the cost he would have to pay to make this wish come true. He also thought of Ariel and living a life on the coast with no worries of being shot. Marshall knew the answer to Eros's question now.

"I want to be out of the killing business once and for all, Eros. Before coming here, I just killed enemy Soldiers and I could still sleep at night. I wouldn't be able to sleep again with this task."

"Your definition of an enemy Soldier is a man with a gun pointed toward you. That's just not how things work my friend. An enemy Soldier is anyone that does not worship the same leaders as you do. If they are worshipping another leader, they will do what's needed to please that leader. It may not be today or tomorrow, but these people in this restaurant will kill you unless you kill them first. The United States recovering its land is the only way to get out of the killing business."

Marshall was surprised at how poetic Eros actually was and how much passion he held for the United States. Marshall had that much passion for the United States up until recent events.

"I understand what you're saying Eros, but can we make a compromise, Sir?" asked Marshall

"Of course, what is it?"

"I will help you with this mission, and I'll stop being resistant to your authority, but I want to retire after this mission. I don't want to continue my career as a sniper. I want to wake up in the morning and not have to clear my house looking for someone who's trying to kill me. I want to be at peace, and I will be once I leave this lifestyle."

"We can do that, Marshall. The United States will be grateful for this service, and you can be relieved of duty knowing you have helped the country in outstanding ways," said Eros with sincerity.

"I want to have a house of my own on the Pacific," Marshall stated with a smile.

"Ahh, yes. The Pacific Ocean is beautiful, Marshall," said Eros with excitement.

"How about this, Marshall. After this mission is completed, and there are no more threats to be offered from Billings, you will be more than welcome to retire. I'll get you on the first train heading west. This job will be paying much better than what you have been currently getting paid. You'll be able to buy a house right next to the ocean, my friend. You just need to persevere over the next few months, and you'll be free to do as you please."

"Thank you, Sir. I'm ready to become an Elitist," said Marshall.

"Fantastic!" yelled Eros as he grabbed his glass of water and held it up to Marshall. Marshall grabbed his drink, and they clinked their glasses together.

Marshall felt persuaded that maybe these people were all threats. They may not be homicidal threats, but they were definitely political threats to the United States and needed to be stopped. Marshall still would only shoot at targets he felt needed to be killed but kept that to himself, not knowing what kind of targets Eros was going to have Marshall shoot.

The two of them finished their breakfast, left some Madison money on the table, and walked to the door. Eros gave a quick wink to Julie and proceeded to leave.

"She's a freak," whispered Eros to Marshall as Eros chuckled.

Marshall could tell Eros was still a little odd but felt more comfortable working with him knowing he cared so much about his country.

"Now that you know the target, you want to head back and start working with the team?"

"Yes, Sir."

"Wonderful, well let's get back so I can teach you how we ambush and eliminate all of these cabins in the surrounding area like we do. We need to destroy all outposts, trails, and cabins surrounding Billings so no word of the destruction of Billings can travel. You understand?" asked Eros.

Marshall knew this was the moment of truth, and there was no going back at this point. Marshall was an Elitist now, and his job was to kill anyone who was a potential threat to the United States.

"Yes, Sir."

CHAPTER 7

Crossing Trails   *May 3, 2046*

A s Marshall and Eros left Billings and headed back to their camp, Eros looked at his phone and saw a message from Ares. Eros and Marshall were at the tree line between the outskirts of town and where the woods started.

"Hey, Marshall, you ready to finally shoot some of these shits up here?" asked Eros with a joyful smile consuming his face.

"Yes, Sir."

"Good, because Ares was scouting just north of here for trade routes and he encountered some Canadians carrying supplies to this city. We're not going to let them get here. Understood?"

"Yes, Sir."

"All right, I hope you're as athletic as you look," said Eros as he ran into the woods. Marshall followed Eros through the woods as they ran halfway to their hideout. In the middle of the woods, with trees surrounding them on all sides, Tar, Themis, and Nyx appeared. Themis handed Marshall his sniper rifle. Marshall gave a nod of thanks and looked toward Eros, who was looking at a map with Tar.

"Okay, you killers, this is the plan," said Eros as he threw the map on the ground and pointed to different locations.

"Ares is positioned in a tree just a mile south of the team traveling. Ares reports there are three horses dragging wagons of food to the city. There are seven men in total. Three riding horseback and four men with assault rifles walking near the horses. The group is obviously not worried about attacks, because they're walking in a semi-trenched pathway, so much so we'll have the high ground. Marshall, you will climb the tree on the left side of the road because Ares is in a tree on the right side. You two will fire the first shots killing the front two riflemen. Nyx and Themis come from behind as everyone is look-ing in the trees and shoot the two back rifleman. Tar and I will kill the lead horse and the horse in the caboose. Snipers will then kill the two riders. We leave this one alive Marshall for questioning. Guns will be on him, and if he looks to shoot, don't hesitate to kill."

Marshall looked at him in complete confusion as he wondered where the crazy guy inside Eros was. Marshall understood why Eros was chosen for this job. He was not only a murderer but also tactical about doing so. The General made the right choice when Eros was picked to lead this team.

"Marshall, quit looking at me with that dumb ass look on your face. Do you understand your role? This will be a good first test for you before we train you on cabin breaching. Let's get moving."

The team of five ran north. All members including Themis ran well, which was surprising to Marshall due to his size. All weapons brought for this trip were silenced. Every weapon used by the Elitist was a silent weapon. Elitists did not have numbers on their side, but they did have the element of surprise. The Elitists also had superior technology compared to citizens of the Outliers

The team ran through the lush woods that surrounded them, no sight of another human even close to them. Marshall looked around to see how isolated they really were for just being a mile or two away from Billings. Marshall saw a small cabin and stared. Tar was running behind Marshall and noticed.

"They're all dead," yelled Tar from behind Marshall.

"You guys cleared this cabin?"

"You know it, Marshall."

"Only cabins left to clear are the ones south of Billings. We figured there was less foot traffic there and we could wait to destroy them until last. There are only three cabins south of Billings anyway from our scout trips," said Tar who started to become short of breath. The running was beginning to be too much for him.

Marshall ran to catch up to Eros, who was now stopped and staring off into the woods ahead. Marshall and Tar caught up to Eros and the others. Eros turned around, walked toward Tar in a fast pace with a serious look, and stared toward Tar. Eros then grabbed Tar's shirt collar with a fierce grip as Eros threw a right hook across Tar's face knocking him to the ground. Eros then angrily approached Marshall.

"I'll let this slide for you because you're new, but don't fucking speak when a mission begins. You are a predator. You need to kill and that's the only thing you'll think about. Tar is a chatter box, who I've warned several times."

"I'm sorry, Sir," said Marshall as Tar stood. Tar held his chin and pushed his jaw back into place as the team heard the click.

Tar and Eros held a rage filled stare until Tar looked elsewhere. He knew there was not much he could do in this situation.

A smile emerged from Eros.

"See, now we can all be friends. Just follow my rules, and I'll be your friend. Right Tar?" Eros spoke these words with a sarcastic tone that came across as someone who was crazy.

"Yes, Sir," said Tar.

"Good. Now let's keep moving."

Just as fast as this event happened, the team was off running again. Marshall looked at Tar who still looked at the ground, ashamed of being thrown down by just one punch.

★ ★ ★

Ares sat in a tree overlooking the pathway, which was dirt with no trees in the radius of the path. This was an opportune situation for the Elitists. Tons of cover for them as the enemy walked a path with no cover or knowledge about what was about to happen.

Eros slowed down as he looked at his GPS and saw Ares, who marked his area. Eros gave the hand signal to slow down and crouch. Eros called the team to huddle behind the bush that was just 500 feet away from the tree in which Ares was hidden.

"Marshall, you need to move now because their convoy will be able to see you cross the path soon. So pick a tree with good sight and set up," said Eros.

"Yes, Sir," said Marshall who left the huddle and hid behind the tree that Ares was using on the east side of the pathway.

"Don't fuck this up, noobie," whispered Ares making himself laugh.

Marshall did not bother to acknowledge him, because he was now only focused on the mission in front of him. Marshall looked behind the tree to see if the convoy had made it to a visible range, but they had not. Marshall ran from the top of the trench on the east side of the path to the pathway and exited on the west side tree line. Marshall grabbed his tree pegs from his pack and stabbed the pegs into the tree to climb to the top.

Marshall steadied his gun on a tree branch in front of him while he crouched at the top of the tree base. The leaves left him invisible to people passing but gave Marshall a perfect shot and camouflage. Marshall saw his phone light up and looked. There was a check box of either, "yes" or "no", and at the top of the box was the question, "Ready to fire?"

Marshall clicked, "yes", and looked down the sight of his sniper rifle. Marshall had done this a million times and was ready to show his team that they made the right choice. Marshall was also excited to defend his country again after the issues on the train.

In the distance, Marshall saw the first horse appear in his sights. Marshall waited until all members of the convoy were in shooting distance. Just as Ares described, there were four men walking on the corners of the convoy, occasionally looking into the woods. It was amateur work, and Marshall knew these men were no challenge for this team. The last horse continued past the bush in which Themis and Nyx where hiding. Marshall felt a vibration on his phone and knew that was the signal to fire.

His scope was already on the man in the front left corner of the convoy. Marshall had a clear chest shot. Marshall exhaled and gently pulled the trigger. The bullet fired out of the gun, instantly killing the man and knocking him backward. At the same exact second, Ares shot his rifle and aimed for the rifleman in the front right, shooting the man in the face causing the rifleman's whole body to jerk backward.

Themis and Nyx fired their silenced assault rifles at the two riflemen in the back, killing them instantly. Eros and Tar then fired their assault rifles at the front horse and the horse in the back of the line. The two horses collapsed to the ground causing the men on board to lose their balance. Marshall then took aim at the man in front and fired. The man was shot directly in the center of his chest, just as Marshall had been trained, killing the man instantly. Ares fired at the man on the horse in the back, hitting him in the head.

"Don't move your hands," yelled Eros from a bush just right of the only man left alive.

The surviving man was in awe of the fact that six of his friends were just killed in front of him in less than a few seconds. The horse he was riding could not keep still, so he tried to calm the horse. Ares received a vibration from his phone knowing that was a kill order and Ares sniped the horse in the head causing blood to splatter all over the rider. The horse collapsed, falling to the right and crushing the rider's leg.

The rider screamed horrifically as Themis and Nyx walked closer to him. Nyx disarmed the rider of his pistol as Themis lifted the horse up enough for the rider. The rider crawled out from underneath the horse to relieve some of his pain. The Soldiers head was faced down in defeat while he crawled away, but Nyx kicked him in the face. Blood spurted from his nose as it broke instantly; the rider screamed again. Themis let the horse's body flop to the ground. Nyx gave a hand signal saying the area was clear. Eros and Tar left the tree line and walked to the middle of their destruction.

Eros knelt on the ground and grabbed the man's shirt, aggressively pulling the rider face- to-face, leaving just a few inches between them.

"What's your name?" asked Eros.

The rider was stuttering due to the trauma to his face and fear started to engulf him.

"Rrrrrick, Sir."

"Well, Rrrrrick," said Eros mocking the rider.

"I have some bad news for you unless you can answer some questions."

"I'll answer anything, but please just let me go home."

"Of course, of course, Rick. I'm not a savage," said Eros in a sarcastic tone everyone in his team recognized.

While the integration continued, Marshall inspected the area, thinking this had been too easy. Something did not feel right, so Marshall searched the tree line. His eyes were wide open, patrolling the area like a hawk, looking for the slightest movement.

"Where are you coming from, Rick?"

"I'm from a city on the Canadian border," said Rick in a panic as tears ran down his face in fear.

"How many people you estimate live there?"

"At least a couple thousand."

"Hmm. I guess my team can't kill that many people now, can we Rick?"

"It's a lot of people, Sir."

As Rick answered Eros, Eros punched Rick in the face and a smile emerged on Eros's face again.

"That was the wrong answer, my friend. Have you seen my team? We're pretty awesome, wouldn't you agree?"

Rick just shook his head rapidly, because he did not want to risk another wrong answer.

The interrogation continued for another two minutes and Marshall grew more worrisome. Marshall could not see any enemies, but just had a hunch they were being tracked. Marshall did one final scan and saw a quick movement about 300 feet away from where Eros stood. The movement was fast and could have been an animal. Marshall knew an animal would never move toward a group of people like that. Marshall went to his phone and sent a vibration to Eros. Eros looked to his phone and then looked back up at Marshall who was pointing to where he saw movement.

Eros turned his head into the direction at an opportune moment, just in time to see an enemy Soldier crouching in a bush. Eros and Tar rolled over the top of the wagon to get cover from the incoming bullets. Themis and Nyx ran toward the west side of the pathway where the Soldier was just spotted and hid at the base of the hill, unable to be seen by the Soldier. The Soldier opened fire, his machine gun fired at the wagon Eros and Tar were using as cover.

Eros started talking to himself and Tar overheard.

"The fuckers planned this. They knew we couldn't pass up on a free killing of a convoy," said Eros with a displeased, confused look on his face.

A Soldier on the east side in the tree line approached Tar and Eros. As they raised their weapons, the Soldier fell to the ground. Marshall had just sniped the man running to the bushes.

"The fuckers didn't plan on our aces," said Eros with an evil smile toward Tar.

Tar gave a nod of agreement. Ares sniped the first Soldier spotted, who was reloading. Nyx and Themis stood and ran to the tree line where the Soldier had just been killed. Tar and Eros did the same on the east side. Eros sent a message to Marshall. Marshall felt the vibration and looked to see what it said.

"Kill gimp," read the message.

Marshall aimed his scope toward Rick who was laying on his stomach with his hands over his head for protection. Rick was completely unarmed and Marshall knew he was not a threat. Marshall normally would not shoot, but he gave his word to Eros that he would work with no questions asked. Marshall knew with every kill, he would be one-step closer to getting away from this lifestyle and closer to bringing pride to his nation. This was the thought process of a man like Eros but not Marshall.

Marshall was now entirely overcome by Eros's persuasion, treating everyone as an enemy. Marshall wanted freedom, and Eros convinced him listening to orders was the only way to achieve this. Marshall took aim at Rick and thought for a second of what was occurring. Marshall left his conscience behind and shot Rick in the head. Rick's body fell limp.

Themis, Nyx, Tar, and Eros all retreated as Ares and Marshall stayed in the trees providing safety for the ground team. No other troops were seen. Either the troops saw the devastation the Elitists brought to combat, or there were no other troops left to fight.

As Eros walked away, he looked to Tar.

"Plant the flame charge while you have sniper support," said Eros.

Eros turned to Themis and Nyx who were now standing by the wagon.

"Us three are heading back to camp now. Snipers and Tar come back once Tar has planted the charges so it shouldn't be long."

The three left the path and began their walk home. Tar went to the supplies in the middle cart. Tar found several bags of corn. He reached into his bag and pulled out a flame charge. The flame charge was attached to a string, and when the string was pulled to a certain point, the charge would explode. The explosion was different from a normal bomb as there was no sound and only flames were created. This provided quieter kills. Tar placed the charge under the first bag of food and then gently laid the food back on top of the charge. The string was attached to the bag on top and when pulled, fire would engulf a ten-foot radius.

Tar planted one charge in each of the three wagons and then signaled to Ares and Marshall he was set to go. Tar walked toward the safe house as Ares and Marshall each took one last check to see if anyone was watching them. Both snipers felt the area was clear and climbed down from their trees and began their walk to the safe house.

A few hours passed until they arrived at the safe house. Tar, Marshall, and Ares took their time on the walk and decided stealth was better than speed in this situation. For the first time since Marshall arrived, Tar was quiet, and Ares was not speaking poorly of someone else. The three were completely silent because now, they realized they were not invincible.

The three approached the tree with the hollowed-out trunk. They opened the trunk and then opened the vault, which lead to a ladder that went twenty feet below the ground. All of them climbed down the ladder. Ares was the last down the ladder. He shut the tree trunk door and locked the vault closed.

Marshall climbed down the ladder first and turned around to see Eros sitting in the center room at the center table. There was blood all over his knuckles.

Eros stared at the map in front of him. The map was of Billings and the surrounding area. There appeared to be about twenty spots that had an x-mark through them. There were three spots that were simply circled.

All six members of the Elitists stood in the center room, waiting for the briefing from Eros. He looked as if he needed to speak. Eros's eyes scanned each and every member of the team for a few seconds, and then he looked back down towards the map.

"We've taken too long to clear these cabins and attack the city," said Eros.

"I'm sorry, Marshall, that you don't get more time to train with us. But you performed perfectly today. You may have saved my life today and I'm very thankful for you. Those men that attacked us were camouflaged and knew we'd be coming. I knew we'd get caught, but I didn't think they would organize an attack against us. According to our scout missions, there are only three cabins left in the surrounding area. One week from today we're taking out all cabins left around here."

"It's about fucking time," chanted Ares.

Eros looked at Ares with a glare of hate but continued his speech.

"The General is planning the invasion two and a half weeks from today. That means on that day the bombs will go off destroying the city. All cabins will have been cleared by then providing no worries for the incoming troops."

"Why are we even waiting two weeks? Let's just blow the shit town up now and move onto the next mission," yelled Ares, who had become noticeably stressed with this mission.

"Have you ever played any kind of strategy game, Ares? Everything happens in a specific time frame that the General is setting up. Everything needs to happen at exactly the right moment for this mission to be successful," said Eros in a condescending tone.

"I thought the mission was just destroying the town?" asked Marshall, now confused about what was occurring.

"It is and it isn't. Our job is that simple. We're going to blow up the town, and this mission will be over. We're to kill anyone that poses a threat to the U.S. and that's the Outliers, Canadians, and any Madison. Destroying this city will end a trade route that's keeping these people alive. There's a second part of the mission but you'll be long gone by then Marshall, so don't worry."

Marshall was unclear of what would be happening after they cleared the city of all threats. He thought this mission was to exterminate all members of Madison and anyone who was helping them. There seemed to be another part to this mission that no one felt obligated to tell him.

Marshall nodded to Eros knowing he should not ask any more questions. Eros continued with the attack plan.

"We're splitting into two teams to make this go faster. Tar, Marshall, and I will take the cabin closest to us and will head to the city directly after, planting bombs the rest of the day. Nyx, Themis, and Ares will head to the middle cabin where you will kill all of them and camp there overnight. According to our scouting, this cabin has several shift changes on a regular basis, so you three will be camped there picking off any wanderers. You three will stay there for at least two days and then head to the last cabin and end them."

The team knew this was a good plan and it would work. Marshall knew that with every step closer to perfecting this mission, he was one-step closer to being relieved from this duty. Marshall felt betrayed by not knowing the true intentions of this mission. However, he would not disobey orders, again. He kept his mouth shut and nodded toward Eros to acknowledge he understood.

"Marshall, this coming week, I'll train you on our signals, strategies, and all that fun stuff. After that, though, we'll attack the cabin and then head to Billings to plant some bombs. Following that, you'll have to wait one week for the bombs to go off. Finally then you're free from working here anymore. If you would like, you can get some sleep. Please go ahead, because I need to talk to the rest of the team who are staying on board for phase two."

"Yes, Sir," said Marshall, who walked to his room.

"Deserter," whispered Ares as Marshall passed him.

Marshall walked on, not acknowledging Ares and shut the door behind him. Marshall was curious what phase two entailed, but understood that if he found out, he would probably have to stay and help. Marshall laid in his bed and tried to think of a happy place to drift away into sleep.

Eros continued talking to the rest of the team.

"General Quartz will have his team of scientists and troops flown in two and a half weeks from today. The city will be destroyed just hours before, so no one will be around. They'll set up the missile launcher over the next few weeks. As you can see on the map, Billings is the center of all bombing pathways whether we choose to fire at Canada or Madison. Marshall can't know of this plan so no one discuss this with him. It took me way too long to just convince him to snipe for me. I don't think he could handle knowing that this was designed for the destruction of an entire civilization. He's not the ruthless Soldier I thought he was, and that's why he's not sticking around for phase two. He's a great shot, but he has too much of a conscience to do what we do."

The team all confirmed they understood their roles over the next few weeks and headed off to bed. All members of the Elitists knew this was the final stretch. Soon all of their hard work would be put into action. The countdown to the end of Billings began.

CHAPTER 8

Welcome Home   *May 5, 2046*

Grandpa woke up around 5 AM and saw his sleeping wife lying next to him. He gave her a big kiss on her forehead and got out of bed. He looked out of the window to see if he could see his three grandchildren coming home, but he was yet to see them.

Grandpa did his walk around the house making sure everything was normal and that everything seemed to be up to his code. Grandpa walked outside to make sure his solar generator was properly working. Grandpa checked the wires leading from the solar panels to the generator, making sure everything would be good for the day. Everything was in order, and it was time to relax in his favorite chair with a cup of coffee.

He turned on the coffee machine and waited for the machine to fill. As Grandpa was waiting, he headed to Tommy's room to make sure he had slept well. Grandpa opened the door a crack and peeped his head in the room. Tommy was sleeping peacefully. He saw something shiny peeking out from underneath Tommy's bed and inspected what it was. It was a scalpel. Grandpa looked at the scalpel in confusion, wondering how Tommy got one of these and why it was underneath his bed.

Grandpa looked back at Tommy to check if he was still asleep and he was. Grandpa then looked under the bed and saw a dead mouse. Grandpa jumped a little at the sight and realized it must have been killed recently since it had not stunk up the house yet. He saw a BB gun wound in the side of mouse. Grandpa put the mouse back under the bed so Tommy did not know he had been snooping. As he was putting mouse away he felt something cold and wet. Grandpa panicked again and pulled his hand back realizing his fingers were covered in blood. He looked at what he touched and saw a mouse tied to a board with its limbs outstretched and its belly cut open entirely.

Grandpa could tell Tommy had done this several times before, as the cut looked like an experienced one.

Grandpa left everything the way he found it, went to the kitchen to wash his hands, and drank his coffee. He sat in his chair contemplating what was going on in Tommy's mind. Tommy had always been different, but things were getting out of hand.

Grandma came through the hallway and into the front room where Grandpa was sitting and gave him a gentle touch on his shoulder.

"Good morning."

Grandpa jumped because he was zoned out and mentally still focused about Tommy.

"Oh, hey, good morning, darling."

"Everything alright? You seem even jumpier than normal," asked Grandma.

"It's Tommy again."

"I told you it's just a stage. He had a traumatic incident happen when he was young. He now has family surrounding him, and he'll come out of his shell soon."

"I don't know. This is topping my scale for what's acceptable."

"What happened?"

"I was checking on him this morning, and I found a scalpel underneath his bed with a mouse he examined last night," said Grandpa with fear in his voice.

"Are you serious?" Grandma said as she stared at Grandpa from the kitchen with a disgusted look on her face.

"How do you want to handle this?" asked Grandma.

"I think we should confront him today, and ask him what he's doing with this stuff. We need to get to the bottom of this before something really bad happens."

"Sounds like a good plan to me, dear. For now let's try to relax and enjoy the nice weather."

Grandma poured herself some coffee and walked over to the couch where she always lounged each morning to do her morning routine.

"I just love the smell of your chair," joked Grandma.

"It's just a mustier version of myself," said Grandpa with a smile.

"That's why I love it. You are always stinking up the house even when you're out hunting or doing whatever you have to do for the day."

"We've been together for forty years now. Sooner or later you'll get tired of this smell."

"Never," said grandma with a smile and some sass.

"Let's hope the kids get back today, too. There's just too much for me to be stressed about right now," said Grandpa.

"You need to relax, dear. The kids know how to take care of themselves, and we'll talk to Tommy later. So please, just relax."

Grandpa did just that. He drank his coffee and tried to get his mind off all of his stresses. A few hours passed, and Tommy finally opened his bedroom door. Grandpa and Grandma could hear him heading to the bathroom and doing his own morning routine. Tommy left the bathroom and headed to the kitchen to get some water to drink.

"Good morning, sweetie," said Grandma.

Tommy just smiled toward Grandma, acknowledging her, and continued to be in his own world. Grandpa looked to Grandma with a look of worry and suggested with his eyes they talk to him right now. Grandma began to speak.

"Hey, Tommy? Can you come over here and talk to us about something?"

"What is it?" barked Tommy.

Grandpa spoke up as Tommy spoke to his grandmother in a rude voice.

"I found something in your room, and we need to talk to you about it," stated Grandpa in a serious tone.

Tommy walked to the front room from the kitchen and stood in front of them. He looked at his grandparents with disgust.

"Where did you get a scalpel?" asked Grandpa.

"You snooped in my room?" yelled Tommy.

"It's not snooping when you're my grandchild. I care about you. So please tell me. How did you get the scalpel?"

"I bought it from some guy in Billings, if you have to know," yelled Tommy who stormed off toward his room. Grandpa started to yell because Tommy was out of hearing distance.

"Why did you cut open a mouse last night?"

Tommy stood frozen at the knowledge of being caught.

"Why did you feel the need to cut open the mouse?"

Tommy started walking back toward the front room. Grandpa and Tommy stood in front of each other in the hallway.

"I just wanted to see what was inside."

"We have tons of science books here, Tommy. I taught you about anatomy basics just a couple weeks ago. You didn't need to kill the mouse and play operation on it."

"I don't see what the big deal is. You've killed people before. What's so wrong with killing a useless mouse?"

"I kill people because they threaten me or my family. How did this mouse threaten your life?"

"It's weaker than me, so what does it matter?"

"Because, Tommy, you just can't kill things that are weaker than you. You need to respect nature and all things that inhabit it."

Tommy stared at Grandpa with rage in his eyes. Grandpa stared straight back.

"Why don't you just leave me alone and mind your own business?"

"You're my responsibility, so I need to be in your business to make sure you're growing up right."

Tommy rolled his eyes, turned his back to his grandpa, and headed back to his room.

"You need to respect your grandparents, Tommy," yelled Grandpa.

Tommy continued to his room and whispered under his breath. "You'll be weaker than me someday." Tommy proceeded to slam his door.

Grandma saw how angry Grandpa was, walked over to him, gave him a hug, and tried to calm him.

"Why won't he talk to us? Why's he doing such weird stuff?" yelled Grandpa as he tried to shake off his anger.

"I don't know, darling, but we need to keep trying. Tommy needs us even if he doesn't understand that yet."

Tommy sat on his bed with his scalpel in his hand, staring at it and the two dead mice on the ground. Tommy stood up and walked toward his closet. He knelt down and lifted up a floorboard to find dozens of mice trapped in a cage. He reached into the cage and pulled out a mouse. Tommy gently petted the mouse and the mouse became less fidgety. Tommy then grabbed the scalpel and laid the mouse flat on its back. Tommy cut the mouse down the center of its chest all the way to the beginning of its tail. The mouse squirmed while it was still alive, but eventually stopped moving. Tommy felt a wave of relief take over his body once the mouse stopped moving. He watched all of the blood pour out onto a rag he always laid out for these circumstances.

Several hours passed since the argument in the hallway. Tommy cleaned up his dead mice and hid them away. Tommy started reading a book in his room.

Grandpa was outside checking to see if any of the traps had been triggered and to see what they would be cooking for dinner. Grandma checked their fishing trap to see if they had caught any fish. The cabin was surrounded by trees with a small pond just a half a mile away.

Grandpa was checking his last trap, which was out of view of the cabin when he saw a truck approaching him. Grandpa grabbed his shotgun and hid behind the tree closest to him. He took aim at the vehicle. The people inside the truck drove closer and Grandpa realized it was his grandchildren. Happiness grew across his face. Grandpa came out of cover and ran toward the truck. The truck stopped, Natalie, Jerrod, and Omar all ran to Grandpa and gave him a hug.

"I've missed you kids so much!" exclaimed Grandpa with pure joy.

"We were only gone for a few days, Grandpa. No need to miss us too much," said Jerrod with a smile on his face.

"Well, I was just worried about you guys, but I'm so happy you're all back. You found a working truck?" asked Grandpa in excitement.

"We found a lot more than that!" said Omar with enthusiasm.

Grandpa walked over to the trunk and opened some of the boxes, finding ammo and canned food, much to his delight.

"You three did it!" yelled Grandpa who was happy about them completing their first mission. This was proof that he trained them well enough to survive in the world.

"Well, I'm going to drive the truck to the cabin, and we can start unpacking," said Omar.

"I haven't been in a vehicle in years. Mind if I join you?" asked Grandpa.

"Of course not," exclaimed Omar.

The two jumped into the driver and passenger's seat and drove to the cabin. Jerrod and Natalie started walking toward the cabin holding hands.

"Well, we made it home, Natalie. I hope you're still into me after all of your traveling," joked Jerrod.

"There was this guy in California who just had magical lips. In the end though, he just had too perfect of a tan. I need my man to have a wonderful farmer's tan," said Natalie in a sarcastic tone with a grin.

Jerrod gave Natalie a flirtatious smile and lifted his sleeves up to show his tan lines.

"Jerrod, please, we're in public. Don't get me going too much."

"Why not?" asked Jerrod who turned to her and picked her up off the ground and kissed her. The two smiled at each other.

"I love you, Jerrod."

"I love you, Natalie."

The two continued staring at each other a little longer and kissed but knew they both had work to do.

"Let's help our family unload the truck first and talk to Tommy, because you haven't seen him in a few days," suggested Natalie.

"You're right," said Jerrod while kissing Natalie's cheek.

Jerrod and Natalie reached the cabin and saw Grandma giving Omar a far too lengthy hug. Omar knew never to end one of Grandma's hug so he just continued to embrace. Jerrod and Natalie pointed and laughed as Omar mouthed to them, "You're next," with an evil smile.

Grandma saw Natalie and Jerrod. Grandma gave Omar one last big kiss on his forehead and ran as fast as she could over to Natalie and Jerrod. Grandma injured her leg a few months back by falling down, and it had not healed properly. As a result, she limped around anywhere she went.

"You two are back!" yelled Grandma with excitement.

Grandma hugged them both at the same time in a big group hug between the three of them.

"I love you two so much, and I'm so happy you're back."

"I love you, too, Grandma," said Natalie.

"Love you, too, Grandma," echoed Jerrod.

The hug continued for at least another minute as Grandma soaked in the love she had been missing over the past few days.

"Darling, could you let them breathe so they can help Omar and me finish unpacking?" asked Grandpa.

"Fine. But don't be surprised if all of you get sneak-attack hugs later," said Grandma.

Grandma went back inside to lay down on her couch and to rest her leg. Grandpa and the kids continued to unload the car. Tommy had not come out to see his brother and friends yet.

"Is Tommy good Grandpa?" asked Jerrod.

"We got into a little bit of a fight this morning so things have been tense in the house."

"What was the fight about?"

"It's nothing to concern you, Jerrod. Just kids being kids."

"All right, just making sure he's good."

"Well, I want to see the little guy," said Omar as he entered the cabin and walked toward Tommy's room. Omar knocked on the door. Omar and Tommy shared this room, as it was the biggest, and it had two twin beds. The other two bedrooms just had enough room for one queen bed each. Natalie and Jerrod shared, and so did Grandpa and Grandma.

"Can I come in, bud?" asked Omar.

"Yeah," said Tommy with sadness controlling his voice.

"How've you been, Tommy?"

Tommy shrugged his shoulders as he lowered the book he was reading.

"What's wrong, bud?"

"Grandpa yelled at me this morning for no reason. I think he's losing it."

Omar laughed and continued to speak. "Grandpa's not losing it. He was probably just stressed. What did he yell at you about?"

"I made this room really messy while you were gone, and he just went off on me."

"Aww, I'm sorry, buddy, that he did that. I think if you just apologize to him now, that would make his day. I see you cleaned the room, too, so there's nothing to be upset about anymore."

"I guess so."

Omar took the book from Tommy and said, "Come on let's tell him now and you can say hi to your brother and Natalie."

"Fine."

Omar laughed at Tommy's stubbornness and pulled him from the bed. The two walked downstairs to the hallway. Grandma saw the two of them walking together and was hit with some happiness to see Tommy socializing. Natalie saw Tommy and went to give him a hug.

"Hey, Tommy, hope you didn't miss me too much," said Natalie.

"Oh, don't worry about that," said Omar as he looked toward Natalie.

Tommy did not respond to Natalie, but gave her a welcoming smile to make her feel accepted. Tommy then faced Grandpa, who stood in the doorway.

"I'm sorry about earlier, Grandpa. It was just early, and I wasn't really awake so I just came off as cranky."

Grandpa knew Tommy was lying to his face about his apology. But everyone else in the family believed him, so Grandpa played along.

"It's okay, Tommy. Sorry I lost my temper, too."

"See? Now we're all one big happy family again," said Omar.

"Amen, son," said Grandma from the couch.

The family finished unpacking and parked the truck a half mile away from the cabin. The family hid the truck between some large and bushy trees. Grandpa assumed that thieves could not steal what they did not know was there. Grandma caught some fish in the pond earlier in the day. The family also opened some of the canned food as they celebrated their successful mission. All six members of the family ate at the table in the kitchen and joked around with each other as Omar told stories about their adventure.

Jerrod looked to Natalie with nervous eyes and Natalie looked right back with reassuring eyes, giving him a nod.

"Hey, Grandpa, I need to ask you something," stated Jerrod.

"What's on your mind, Jerrod?"

"On our drive home from our mission, the three of us were talking and all of us want to join the Madison Legacy."

"You're already part of it. All of you are already part of it," said Grandpa with some confusion as he looked toward Grandma.

"I know we are, but we want to be Soldiers for the army. We want you to train us like you trained my dad. You've given us the basics to survive against an enemy, but Omar, Natalie, and I want to know everything you can teach us."

There was complete silence around the table as Grandpa sat thinking of what to say.

"The war's over, kids. There were dangerous people out there, I know, but the war is over."

"No, it's not Grandpa, and you know that. You can't act like you haven't heard the rumors of the murders happening around Billings. Who knows when those people will be here? I told Omar not to tell this story yet but we saw a mercenary get off the train when we boarded. Something big is coming, and the three of us want to be as ready as we can be."

"How do you even know he was a mercenary?"

"He killed three men with no hesitation or difficulty. He got off the train where we got on. There's a good chance he's around here. Who knows who else is around here?" asked Jerrod as he became more frustrated while he spoke.

"What happens after I train all of you?" asked Grandpa.

"We plan to head to Madison's capital and enlist in the army there. They won't provide the one-on-one training that you can offer Grandpa, and you know that. You're a retired Madison academy trainer. You know how to make us all even better shots and how to be even stronger."

"Omar and Natalie? You both want to join the army, too?"

Natalie spoke first. "I saw my parents die six years ago, and all of you treated me like family. I couldn't be more grateful. I just need to serve a purpose for my life, and I believe it's fighting the States and making the future better for when I have kids. Eventually, this cabin will not be big enough for all of us."

"I have the same story as Natalie. My parents died by the States and I want to defend any other fellow Madisons," Said Omar

"Well, if that's what the three of you want, then I guess I'll do that for you guys. I have heard of the cabin raids happening just east of Billings, and it's been worrying me. Maybe you're right, Jerrod, maybe it's time all of you are trained to one hundred percent."

"I want to be trained, too," said Tommy.

Tommy did not usually speak at dinnertime. The family all stared at him and then looked at Grandpa for his response. The family knew Grandpa had been hesitant to train Tommy and were unaware of what the response could be.

"And you will be, Tommy. I think it's time you come with us on these training sessions."

Tommy smiled, looked back at his plate, and continued eating.

"Things are going to be different this time, though. To become a good shot, you need to fire thousands of rounds and not just shoot a deer every once in a while around the cabin. I know you, Jerrod, are an ace shot and have that award to prove it but the rest of you need a lot of practice. Shooting that many rounds around here will cause too much commotion. We need to head to the mountains to practice in private," said Grandpa.

"The mountains?" asked Omar.

"I trained all of your parents in the mountains west of here. Great target areas and no one lived there at the time. I'm sure no one moved in since then. If we're in the mountains, we can shoot freely and make all of you aces. I'm going to teach you how to counter-fight enemies, how to make a quick small bomb and how to use any weapon you could possibly hold."

"I can't make it to the mountains with you guys," said Grandma.

"I just can't breathe up there, and I had issues when I was there years ago. I'm sure it's worse now."

"I'm not leaving you, darling."

"Yes, you are. These four in front of us are the future of Madison and who better to train them than you?"

"There are murderers out there killing people in cabins, and you want all of us to just leave you here?" asked Grandpa angrily.

"Exactly. There are murderers out there, and you have trained them decently so far, but they need the expert course now. It's about time these kids asked you to finally go train, and you'll do just that. We now have enough ammunition to train them, too. Everything is lining up so don't you dare miss this opportunity. I'll be right here when all of you get back, and you'll see that no one attacked the cabin. Besides, I'll blow anyone away who walks in the door and you know that," said Grandma.

"Okay," said Grandpa.

The four kids became ecstatic. They realized they would finally be trained by the legend himself. Grandpa and Grandma stared at each other across the table, while Grandpa worried extensively about being away from his wife.

"Tomorrow I'll show you how to build a safety stealth trench and how to set some traps around the cabin. This will be your first lesson. Then we'll drive out to the mountains tomorrow night."

Omar, Natalie, and Jerrod thanked Grandpa for agreeing to train them, and all spoke about what the mountains could entail. Grandpa lost focus with the conversation and stared toward Tommy who was not speaking anymore but just gently poking the fish head that was left on his plate from dinner. Tommy caught Grandpa staring and stared back for a second. He then left the table and headed toward his room.

"This will be good for him, Grandpa. He needs some family time, and it's healthy he's included," said Jerrod.

Grandpa laughed a little and spoke. "I sure hope you're right and ready for what's about to come."

"I am," said Jerrod with confidence.

CHAPTER 9

Defense   *May 6, 2046*

Grandpa woke up to the sunshine peering through the window as the sun started to rise. He looked over to his beautiful wife who was still asleep. He kissed her on the forehead and was just about to begin his normal morning routine.

Today was a tad different; because it was the last day he would see his wife for the next two weeks. The two had spent every day together for the last six years until now. Grandpa was worried about his wife and that kept him awake at night. He knew the next two weeks would not be easy. Instead of getting out of bed and beginning his day, Grandpa decided to lay in bed a little longer and cherish the minutes he had to lay with her.

An hour passed and Grandma awoke.

"Good morning! You feeling all right?" asked Grandma with her eyes half open and a deep morning voice.

"Yeah, why'd you ask?"

"Because you haven't laid in bed with me in the morning since the day we were married," said Grandma as she laughed.

"I'm just making up for lost time, that's all."

Grandpa and Grandma smiled at each other.

"You know you're worrying for nothing, right?" questioned Grandma.

"I know, but it would be weird not to worry about you."

"Please don't worry about me, darling. If either of us go, you know the other one won't have to wait too long at our age," Grandma said with a laugh.

Grandpa and Grandma continued talking and enjoying each other's company as the hours slipped away from them. The two finally decided to get out of bed and headed downstairs. Omar was sitting at the dining table eating eggs.

"I'm up before you, Grandpa. What's wrong with the world now?"

Grandpa cracked a smile and said, "You ready for everything today?"

"I'm ready to train and have open ears to whatever else you need to inform me about."

"Great answer, Omar. Where's everyone else?"

"Tommy is reading in his room, and Jerrod and Natalie are still in their bedroom."

"Well, I guess we can give them another hour, but then it's time to teach you all how to dig some quick traps and safety holes."

Jerrod laid in bed holding Natalie as they talked throughout the morning. The two held each other and reminisced about funny stories that had happened to them.

"I don't want to get out of bed, Natalie," said Jerrod in a complaining, sarcastic tone.

"Me neither, babe. Let's just forget about this whole joining-the-war thing and lay here for the rest of our lives."

"I could not have said it better myself, Nat."

"We're going to do great things in this world, right Jerrod?" asked Natalie who needed reassurance.

"We are, Natalie. But I just want you to know that not everyone needs to know your name at the end of the day, Nat. There are tons of people in this world who do great things every day, and we'll never know their names."

"I know but wouldn't it be cool to be remembered as the person who ended the U.S. and saved Madison?" asked Natalie with excitement.

"It would be. I'm not denying that. I'm just saying there's more to living a life than other people remembering your name. I know your name, Nat, and everyone in this house knows your name. These are the people who matter. Who cares what anyone else thinks? Don't fight this war for fame and being remembered. Fight because we stand next to each other, and we want our kid to grow up in a world where they're not afraid of being ambushed within this country," said Jerrod in a sincere tone, trying to convince Natalie of his view on the world.

"Grandpa always said that in his day people only cared about fame. The people back then would do weird shit on the Internet and be horribly mean to people that they had never met just to get attention. They were all chasing a goal that really had no prize. Being loved and respected by people you know is my idea of fame, and I really hope you start to see things that way, too. You'll be happier, I promise," said Jerrod as he kissed Natalie on the forehead.

Natalie smiled back at him knowing he was right. Natalie always thought being known by everyone was the purpose and was what brought happiness, but she was wrong.

Grandpa knocked on their door.

"You two ready for today? We got a lot of stuff to do, so let's get a move on it."

"We'll be out in a second Grandpa," yelled Jerrod.

"Ready to become Soldiers of Madison?" asked Natalie with a smile on her face.

"Let's go make some killer traps," shouted Jerrod with excitement toward his pun.

"We can no longer speak to each other," said Natalie as she turned away from him in the bed.

The two began to play wrestle, and Jerrod got on top and held her arms to the bed.

"I love you," said Jerrod.

"I love you, too," said Natalie as they both leaned in for a kiss.

The two knew it was time to get serious. They both got dressed in the appropriate clothing and gear for the day ahead. The pair walked over to the cabinet in their room and grabbed their weapons. Natalie had her shotgun while Jerrod had his sniper rifle. They walked down the stairs into the kitchen and saw Grandma, Grandpa, and Omar sitting at the table.

"Is Tommy still in his room?" asked Grandpa in frustration.

"Relax. I'm sure he's coming down," said Grandma in a calming voice, trying to sooth Grandpa.

"We have stuff to do, and the kid thinks the world revolves around him."

Tommy walked down the stairs just as Grandpa finished speaking.

"You know what? I can hear you Grandpa. I'm sorry I'm such a constant disappointment to you."

"You're not a disappointment, Tommy. I just need you to take this seriously and listen to me. You'll need to listen to me when we're in the mountains, and I need to trust you will."

"I will Grandpa! Just stop riding me for once and just treat me like your other grandkids who you seem to be so nice to," yelled Tommy with hatred in his eyes and tone.

Grandpa stood from the table and walked outside knowing what he would say next would be too mean for Tommy to handle.

"You can't yell at him like that, Tommy. You need to respect him," shouted Grandma.

"He doesn't respect me, so why does it even matter?"

"Because he's your Grandpa, and this week he's your drill instructor, so don't you dare talk to him like you just did."

Tommy did not speak again and shrugged his shoulders. He had nothing left to say to Grandma.

"Hey, we should all get outside to help Grandpa. I think he's starting without us," said Omar.

Out the window, he saw Grandpa was digging.

The four grandchildren walked outside to see Grandpa angrily digging a hole right next to a tree. Jerrod looked to Omar and could tell how much pain Grandpa was in and how he was trying to take his anger out on the dirt.

"Hey, what are you building, Grandpa?" asked Jerrod.

"Well I'm putting a trap right next to this tree. It's a perfect vantage point to shoot toward the cabin and it's where most Soldiers would choose to shoot from. First, you'll want to grab a knife and slice up the top layer of grass. We'll be placing this layer of grass back over the trap so it'll have a very natural look, such that the Soldier won't even think twice about it."

Grandpa continued slicing the grass with his knife and used his shovel to dig underneath the ground.

"Do you want any help, Grandpa?" asked Jerrod as they watched for a few minutes.

"No. This one will be mine. There are shovels on the side of the house and some good gardening knives. Grab those and choose a tree to dig by. I'll check all of your work soon," said Grandpa as he continued working, not even wasting time to meet eyes with anyone.

All four grandchildren walked over to the cabin and each grabbed a shovel and a gardening knife.

"This is a cool looking knife," said Tommy in excitement to Omar.

The knife had a sickle-like blade, so it could get underneath the ground easier. The blade made a "J" shape.

"Yeah, you don't see that every day," said Omar.

Tommy was lost in the knife and could only focus on that one item.

"Well, let's split up around the area, find a good place to dig, and set up the trap," said Jerrod.

The four of them split up and walked to different areas that would be good vantage points to shoot at the cabin. Tommy chose a spot semi-close to Omar. Tommy looked at the patch of grass in front of him and did not know where to start.

"Hey, Omar, before you get too far along with yours, can you help start my hole?"

"Yeah, no problem, bud."

Omar walked over to the spot Tommy chose and got on his knees. He used the gardening knife to get the grass up first. Tommy stood tall over Omar who now knelt near him. Tommy had his gardening knife in hand and looked toward Omar in an odd way. Grandpa was now much farther along than his grandchildren were and was waist deep in his hole. He looked around the area to see how everyone was doing and saw Tommy with the knife in his hand standing over Omar. Fear engulfed Grandpa, and his heart sank.

"You see, Tommy, it's not too hard at all," said Omar.

"You're right, Omar," said Tommy who knelt down with his knife sticking out to the right just enough to clip Omar.

"Ahh! What're you doing, Tommy?" yelled an angered and frustrated Omar.

A small cut was now on Omar's upper arm.

"I'm sorry, Omar, I didn't mean it," said Tommy in a fake panic.

Grandpa saw the whole ordeal and stared at Tommy. Tommy looked up with a slight smile on his face now that Omar started to walk to the house to clean his cut. Tommy looked around a little and made eye contact with Grandpa. Actual panic now overtook Tommy as he immediately stared at the ground and continued to dig.

Grandpa tried to think of what he could do in this situation. How do you handle a kid who gets a thrill from these kinds of things? Would anyone believe him anyway? Why does he feel the need to do these things? Grandpa was panicked but kept a sturdy composure while he continued to dig.

Omar returned from the house after Grandma provided the proper cleaning to Omar's cut. The five of them continued to dig for a few more hours and then all met Grandpa for the next lesson.

"Well, we were able to make a hole that can be covered. This could maybe sprain an ankle but that's not good enough. The holes are about four feet deep so now it's time to add a little extra to these pits," said Grandpa.

Grandpa went behind the tree and pulled out four small, sharp sticks.

"These traps are made to slow down your enemy and make them bleed-out. No more, no less. You could get lucky, and they could fall face first, but it's unlikely. I'm stabbing these four spike-like sticks into the ground and they'll likely puncture a hole in the lower half of your enemy. It'll be difficult for them to leave these holes after they're wounded and that's when someone comes in and does a cleanup."

The traps were very simple but cheap and effective. The four grandchildren knew fighting for the Madisons would require them to fight at a technological disadvantage to the United States.

"Next step is to go find some semi-thick sticks and carve a stake into the sticks with your knife. Then just stab them into the ground and remember where your hole is. Worst thing would be to forget where you made your trap," said Grandpa.

All four grandchildren walked away, finding sticks to use as their stakes. Grandpa reached for Jerrod before he could get too far away.

"Hey, can I speak to you about something?" asked Grandpa.

"Yeah, what's up Grandpa?"

Grandpa pulled Jerrod closer to the house to get out of range of the others.

"Tommy is really beginning to worry me, Jerrod."

"What'd he do this time?"

"Omar was cut, Jerrod. It looked like an accident, but Tommy legitimately sliced his arm. I saw the whole thing. I don't know what to do with him anymore."

"What're you saying, Grandpa?"

"Tommy is not right in the head, Jerrod. He's a threat to us all. I can't believe that I'm saying stuff like this about my own grandchild, but he's not a safe kid," said Grandpa passionately in hopes of persuading Jerrod.

"I believe you, Grandpa," said Jerrod, understanding that this was seriously distressing his grandpa.

Grandpa was so relieved to have someone believe him. Grandma could not accept the fact that Tommy was crazy and the other kids did not know of this issue.

"Thank you, Jerrod. Thank you so very much for believing me."

"I know you wouldn't lie about something like this Grandpa, so don't worry. I'm on your side. It's just, well, what should we do about this?"

"I don't know. If I say anything, Tommy will play the innocent card, and no one will believe me. For now, just watch him like he's a threat. Grandma says the time we spend together in the mountains is just what we need to get through to him. I hope she's right. If things aren't better after the trip, then the whole family will need to speak to him. Just don't give him the benefit of the doubt. Don't trust him, Jerrod," said Grandpa almost as if he was scared for his life from his fourteen-year-old grandkid.

"I'll watch him closer now, Grandpa, and I won't say anything to anyone else until after the trip."

"Good. Well, go find some stakes to put into your pit, and then I'll teach you guys one more thing before we leave for the mountains."

Jerrod did as he was told. He ran off into the woods around his cabin and searched for sticks just like everyone else was doing. Tommy gave Jerrod a stare of curiosity. He worried what Grandpa had just told him.

Tommy knew what was inside of him was odd and out of place, but he just had the need to continue as he did. Tommy received the ultimate rush of satisfaction by seeing others suffer. He knew no one would understand, and he did not expect they would. With that in mind, he still would do what was needed to fulfill his need to cause pain.

All members of the Fairbanks family continued sharpening sticks and placed them in their five trap holes. This took only an hour to finish. There were now five deadly fall-in traps surrounding the cabin.

"Good work, everyone. I'm happy that all of you did this pretty fast. The next step is for safety purposes. We're going to build some safety huts around the cabin that anyone can hide in. This will be good for sneak attacks or for when you're trying to evade the enemy," said Grandpa.

Grandpa walked toward the back of the cabin where a shed was and walked out with about a three-foot long bundle of sticks.

"This is a cover to the holes we're going to be digging. What we're digging are called safeties. You'll dig holes around the area. Then you will place this lid on top of the hole with a layer of grass and leaves on top of this lid. It's fast and a perfect hiding spot for people on the run. The sticks are semi-lose so if anyone walks on them, the enemy won't think twice that there's a hole full of people in the area. These hideouts saved my life multiple times, and I'm sure they will come in handy for your war."

The four grandchildren nodded and walked around the area of the cabin to find the best spot to dig a hole and hideout. Grandpa approved of all of the areas, and the Fairbanks family started to dig. Several hours passed before everyone dug their safeties. Grandpa inspected them to make sure they were deep enough to work properly.

"Good work, everyone. I'm proud of all of you. None of you complained the whole day and just did as you were told. All of you are made to be great Soldiers with attitudes like yours. While all of you were digging, I made the covers for the safeties. Normally I won't help like this during training but we're a tad behind schedule, and we need to leave for the mountains tonight."

Grandpa handed out the covers as they all went to their respected safeties and placed the cover on top. The four grandchildren placed grass and leaves on top of the hole to finalize their safeties.

"The sticks are also loose on the cover so you can move the leaves and dirt on top to look more realistic," said Grandpa proudly as the four grandchildren continued to cover their newly dug safeties.

"I made dinner for everyone. Come on in! You have all worked hard enough today," yelled Grandma from the front of the cabin.

"Looks like everything is set here. Let's go eat and then get on the road," said Grandpa.

Grandpa did one last inspection of the four safeties that were dug, and approved them all for being stealthy enough and large enough for people to use. The four grandchildren ran inside as fast as they could when Grandpa told them they could go. Grandpa laughed to himself as they all ran toward Grandma reminding him his grandchildren were just that. They were children to him still. He would never forget the times they had because he knew their relationship would change once in the mountains.

Grandpa walked into the cabin and saw his grandchildren sitting at the table eating their dinner, as Grandma grabbed more food from the stove. Grandpa continued to the table and sat at the head of the table.

"I hope you guys had a decent day out there," said Grandpa.

"It was great, Grandpa," said Natalie in excitement.

"Yeah, Grandpa, this was something we needed to know how to do, so thank you," said Omar.

"I'm glad I can teach you guys these things. Just wait until we head to the mountains and you'll learn even more."

The Fairbanks continued to eat and enjoy their last supper with the whole family for the next two weeks.

"So you going to miss us, Grandma?" asked Omar.

"Of course, sweetie, I'm going to think of all of you over the next two weeks. It's going to be so quiet around here, which I am just not used to," said Grandma.

"We won't be gone too long," said Grandpa trying to make himself feel better about leaving her.

"Oh, I know. I knew this day was coming, and I'm happy it has. The Fairbanks are all grown up now and will represent Madison very well."

Talk at the dinner table settled down now that everyone realized they were leaving directly after their meal. A gentle tension was in the air as they all realized things would be different on their return and it was time to become Soldiers.

Tommy left the table first because he always ate the fastest. He did not make eye contact with Grandma who was signaling him with her eyes for a hug.

"I'm going to grab my things and throw them in the truck," yelled Tommy who walked toward his room.

"I guess that means it's time to go," said Grandpa whose voice was filled with heartache.

"None of you kids are allowed to the leave the table until you give me a hug and let me tell you how much I love you," said Grandma with a joking yet serious tone.

"Of course, Grandma," exclaimed Omar as he walked over to Grandma and gave her a big hug.

Natalie and Jerrod followed Omar's lead and all received a giant hug from Grandma. They each then went to their rooms to finish packing.

"You going to be ok?" asked Grandma to Grandpa, who was standing in the kitchen cleaning.

"Yeah, I'm just trying to convince myself you'll be completely fine with all of us gone,"

"You know I will be. I fought in the same war you did, and you know I'll be fine."

"That was years ago, and now you have trouble just walking."

"Look, I don't want our last talk for the next two weeks to be an argument. Now tell me you love me, you'll miss me, and that I'll see you in two weeks. Then give me the biggest hug you have ever given," said Grandma sternly.

Grandpa walked over to Grandma who was still sitting at the dinner table. He gave her a hug.

"I love you so much, and I'll miss you so much these next few weeks. I need you to keep me relaxed. You know that, so please be safe."

"I love you, too, and I will miss you so much, too. I will be right here when you come back to calm you right down," said Grandma.

The two held their hug for another minute savoring the time they had left before the trip.

"I'll be sitting in your chair every morning, and it will be just like you are actually here," said Grandma jokingly.

"I'll be sure to stink it up before I leave tonight, just for you."

"My hero," said Grandma as the two kissed.

Grandpa wanted to bring up the incident with Tommy today but did not want to upset Grandma. So he kept his mouth shut, and just enjoyed the moment they shared.

The four grandchildren packed all of their clothing, weapons, ammo, water bottles, and food for the trip in the truck. Grandpa did a final count of everything, making sure they had enough of everything.

"Ok, everyone, go say bye to Grandma one last time before we leave," said Grandpa to all four of his grandchildren standing outside next to the truck.

The truck bed was completely full and so was most of the back seat. Three people would sit in the front, while two would be squished in the backseat with supplies. Grandpa was doing his final check for everything and walked back to the cabin to give Grandma one last hug.

He approached the cabin but looked to the bench outside which held all of the digging equipment from earlier. Grandpa made sure everything was there but could not find one of the garden knives. He looked all over the cluttered table and then looked to the ground. The knife was not there. He immediately panicked, assuming Tommy was doing something he should not be doing. Grandpa ran into the cabin to see Tommy giving Grandma a quick hug.

"See, that wasn't so bad, was it Tommy?" asked Grandma, teasing him.

Tommy rolled his eyes and walked outside passing Grandpa without saying anything. Grandma looked up to see Grandpa.

"You ok? You look like you just saw a monster," joked Grandma.

Grandpa calmed himself, trying to believe Tommy would not hurt anyone in his family. Or at least Grandpa tried to convince himself that, even after the incident with Omar earlier today.

Omar, Natalie, and Jerrod gave Grandma one last hug and headed to the car. Grandpa was at the end of the hug line and went last.

"This will be good for them, and you know this. That's why I want you to go."

"I know," said Grandpa trying to trust Grandma's opinion about Tommy.

"Hey, don't go off track between here and the pond, or you could fall in one of the holes. Okay?"

Grandma nodded her head, the two embraced, and confessed their love. Grandpa gave her a kiss, then smiled, and walked out of the cabin.

Grandpa headed to the truck where the grandchildren were already sitting in their seats.

"I guess you can drive this time," joked Omar toward Grandpa.

Grandpa smiled and got in the driver's seat.

"Well, we should be there in about six to seven hours, so feel free to take a nap. We'll be busy once we get there."

Tommy sat in the seat behind Grandpa and the anxiety being created was overwhelming Grandpa. He did not know if Tommy was going to slit his throat while driving, causing them to crash. Hundreds of thoughts crossed his mind regarding what could go wrong as he drove off into the night.

Jerrod sat next to Grandpa in the front and placed his hand on Grandpa's shoulder.

"It's going to be okay, Grandpa. Just relax. I also know Grandma will be fine, so just focus on the mission," said Jerrod. Grandpa used to tell him this when he was younger.

Grandpa smiled at Jerrod, relaxed, and continued driving west to the mountains to turn his grandchildren into Madison Soldiers.

CHAPTER 10

Madison Training   *May 7, 2046*

The night dragged on into the morning as Grandpa continued driving west to his home-away-from-home. Grandpa trained hundreds of Madison Soldiers in this location due to the privacy provided by the elevation and the lack of civilization surrounding the area. The hike to the top of the mountain was filled with steep slopes. This made traveling to the top difficult without the proper vehicle.

Grandpa, Omar, Natalie, Jerrod, and Tommy were all awake as the mountain became visible. Seeing an area without trees left everyone in the truck confused and the feeling of being exposed. It had been around five years since anyone in the truck had seen an area so bleak of vegetation. Only rocks and rocky hills were in front of them.

"Well, we made it through the night everybody," said Grandpa.

"I was awake the whole time. Omar needs to work on his snoring," said Jerrod.

"It couldn't have been too bad, because I slept just fine," said Omar with a smirk.

"Because that's how that works," said Jerrod.

Natalie was in and out of sleep trying to keep her head up because she wanted to be awake when they arrived. Tommy stared out of the side-window, drifting off into space.

"You ready to get to work, Tommy?" asked Grandpa trying to excite everyone in the truck and to lift everyone's morale for being away from home.

Tommy pretended not to hear Grandpa and remained silent in the backseat, looking out of the window.

"I sure am, Grandpa," said Omar who tried to ease the tension, which was forming in the truck.

"Well, at least someone in the truck is ready," said Grandpa.

The truck continued to climb a rocky hill. The mountain had a carved-out path from being travelled on before by the Madisons. The truck was more than capable of carrying all of the members in the truck up the hill in addition to all of the supplies they brought for the two weeks ahead.

The vehicle pulled into an area that was covered by a rocky dome. It looked like the dome only covered half of the area as the other half just looked into the nearby mountain range. The family was completely covered and hidden from any outsiders. They were high enough and used the dome to their advantage. Many people forgot these mountains existed and were left uninhabited, which benefited the Fairbanks to a great extent.

"All right, start unpacking and setting up your new home for the next two weeks," said Grandpa who stretched after getting out of the truck.

"I forgot how relaxing it is to drive," said Grandpa.

"You drive a lot before the war?" asked Natalie who was helping everyone unpack and unload the truck.

"I drove a car everywhere I went. My job was an hour away from my house so I drove to work every day during rush hour. It was horrible, kids. Driving back in the early 2000s was far from relaxing. It was more of a chore. There were so many impatient drivers that would tailgate your car even if you were going twenty miles over the speed limit. They simply thought their time was more important than everyone else's. The world was a lot faster paced and filled with a lot more self-absorbed people," said Grandpa. He was feeling nostalgic being in this training area. This area brought him back his younger years along with many memories.

"What do you mean by self-absorbed?" asked Jerrod.

"People in that time, really, only enjoyed speaking about themselves and only doing things if it bettered themselves. The times were very selfish, and that's why sometimes I think maybe it was a good thing the Civil War happened. It made citizens realize the world didn't revolve around them. There was a bigger picture than just one person. The war created a need for teams and a need for grouping. Before, it was just everyone for themselves."

"I raised you all to do what's best for group rather than yourselves. Saving ten lives is better than protecting just one. Remember that everyone," said Grandpa as he looked around the group.

Tommy was not paying attention to Grandpa's stories because he simply did not care and was primarily focused on being able to shoot a gun over these next couple of weeks. Tommy was excited to be included in this training but did not feel grateful to Grandpa. He felt Grandpa owed him this training.

The Fairbank's family continued unpacking and all members set up their own tents.

Grandpa crawled out of his tent with an assault rifle.

"Everyone ready to become a master of this gun?"

"You know it," shouted Omar with excitement as the three others crawled out of their tents.

All members of the family had their own assault rifle, thanks to the trip to Whitehall. The Fairbanks walked down the rocky hill where they had set up and headed to a wide trench sheltered by rock walls.

"Wait here," said Grandpa to the kids. He walked to the other end of the trench to set up targets for the family to shoot. Grandpa finished his work and began walking back to his grandchildren.

"Bet my shot gets closer to the bull's-eye than yours," said Natalie to Jerrod.

"Ahh, I'm not sure about that one, Nat. This is an assault rifle, not a shotgun. You may have more trouble with a non-spread shot," said Jerrod to Natalie trying to annoy her.

"Okay, I want all four of you in the proper standing position as this will most likely be the height you'll be shooting at on the move," said Grandpa.

The four kids took aim at the four paper targets positioned at the end of the trench.

"Fire," yelled Grandpa.

All four kids took one shot on their own targets. Tommy was the only one to miss the target completely while the other three hit somewhat close to the center of the target. Tommy's face reddened as embarrassment and jealousy took over for missing his target.

"Don't worry about it, Tommy, this is your first time shooting that gun, so it'll take time," said Grandpa.

Tommy angrily held the gun in the fire position awaiting for Grandpa's next cue to fire. Tommy did not say anything, trying to focus on his task.

"I think your girl hit the target a little closer than you, Jerrod," joked Omar.

"I know I did," said Natalie confidently.

"Let's just see how the next one goes. Beginner's luck," said Jerrod jokingly.

Grandpa said fire again, but this time he threw a firecracker between the kids as they took aim causing Tommy and Natalie to fire before they could get a proper aim on their target. Jerrod and Omar hit their targets perfectly and both looked over to each other and gave an accepting nod and smile.

"Grandpa, what the fuck?" yelled Tommy as he looked toward Grandpa with pure rage in his eyes.

"What did you just say to me? We aren't at home anymore. You're training so show me some respect or you can start walking home now," Grandpa yelled.

"You think your enemy will just be standing there, not firing back at you? They want you dead just as much as you want them dead. Get comfortable with noise and distractions, because that's the only way to become a good Soldier. Now let's try hitting the target this time."

The family practiced throughout the day with the assault rifle. Hours passed and nighttime approached. Their first day of training was completed. Omar preferred today's weapon and ended the first night ahead of everyone else in accuracy with this weapon. Jerrod and Natalie felt confident with this weapon, too. Tommy only hit the target a few times throughout the day. The gun began to weigh too much for the fourteen-year-old, causing his aim to worsen as the day continued.

"I want all of you to climb out of this trench and run this hill ten times. At that point, I'll have dinner cooking for all of us, and you four will have had a good workout for the day. Oh yeah, when you reach the top, be sure to do thirty pushups. You'll all be very fit by the end of this trip," said Grandpa who started his walk up the hill.

"Want to race this time, Natalie?" asked Jerrod jokingly knowing Natalie was terrible with pushups.

"You know I can out run you at least," said Natalie with attitude due to the high stress of the day. The four of them began to run up the hill. Omar spoke.

"Uh, oh, trouble in paradise for the couple of the year?"

"Shut up, Omar," said Natalie sternly.

"Well, damn," joked Omar as Jerrod let out a little laugh. Jerrod found it humorous when Natalie was tightly wound.

Tommy had not spoken since Grandpa yelled at him. He did his laps on the hill in complete silence. He was not as fast as the other three, and he did not possess the strength to do the pushups. The one thing Tommy did have was the ability to lie. Tommy started to think to himself that maybe no one would notice if he told Grandpa he was a lap or two ahead of where he really was.

Time passed as the kids continued running. Jerrod finished first followed by Natalie, Tommy, and finally Omar.

"Whoa, Tommy, good for you for beating Omar up and down the hill," said Grandpa knowing the truth of what had happened. Grandpa watched the whole time and confidently knew Tommy lied about the number of pushups he did and the number of times he ran up and down the hill. Omar did not lie and would have beaten Tommy, if Tommy had counted correctly.

"I'm faster than I look," said Tommy with guilt in his voice.

"You know I don't accept liars at this campfire," said Grandpa as his tone grew serious.

"Stop accusing me of stuff! I did all of my laps. It's not my fault Omar's so slow," yelled Tommy defensively.

"Like hell you out ran me, Tommy," said Omar who was tired of Tommy's attitude.

Tommy angrily stormed off into his tent, skipping dinner, and the campfire with everyone.

Tempers were high due to standing in the same spot all day shooting a gun, lack of sleep from the drive, and lack of food throughout the day.

"Why don't the three of you eat and then we can deal with Tommy," said Grandpa trying to calm everyone's temper.

The four sat on some rocks surrounding the campfire. They ate their canned foods and their tensions slowly vanished as their stomachs filled.

"Hey, Grandpa, can I ask you a question?" asked Natalie.

"Go for it, Natalie."

"Why'd you join the Madisons?"

Grandpa started to reminisce to the times before the country split and when there was only one country within this land. Grandpa remembered the country had always been split, but only recently were there literal walls separating the land.

"The United States was a great idea for a country, but too many shitty people took control and ruined it for everyone."

"How so?" asked Jerrod who was now interested in the conversation.

"Every week there would be a news station broadcasting and giving fame to whoever decided to shoot up a public area. People killed others and hated others just for the color of their skin or who they married. There was so much hate in this country. But since the United States allowed freedom of gatherings and speech to even the most outrageous groups, there was no way to stop the spread of craziness."

"The rich controlled who became in charge and the rich would only empower people that supported their ideas. The system of checks and balances were destroyed as the government became more about who had the most money. The poor had no voice in the world and worked paycheck-to-paycheck to support their families. This is when the turn began, but there were many other reasons why I decided to be a Madison,"

"Like what?" asked Natalie.

"Wow, you kids really want to hear me talk tonight," said Grandpa who felt flattered by their interest.

"Humor died in the early 2000s, too, which was an important reason for why I was not proud to be an American. No one took a joke as a joke. People played victims first saying how the joke offended someone when really it was just making light of an incident or a disgusting stereotype. The people of the United States lost the ability to laugh and the expression that laughter was the best medicine was quite an accurate statement. No humor being allowed made the world way too serious, and I didn't want to live in a world like that."

"Any other reason why you wanted to leave?"

"Well, I was telling you earlier about how self-absorbed the world was. The Internet glorified self-absorbed people. People thought every thought they had was golden. They thought so highly of themselves giving them entitlement, which lead to people being assholes."

Grandpa really started to think of all of the problems that went on before the bombs dropped around the world.

"Shit, even the food we ate back then was a political and money-making machine. They served people disgusting and unhealthy food just to make extra money on the product. They added extra sugar to make customers addicted to those products. To top that, those companies then glorified overweight people on the Internet and told people to accept and embrace their obesity. It was a joke in itself to live during those times. We had distanced ourselves too far from nature, and we became robots. Self-absorbed, fat robots," said Grandpa as he laughed about the situation.

"Leaving the United States was one of the best decisions of my life. I left the Internet, which made me happier, and I became closer with nature. I made eye contact when I spoke to people, instead of texting someone who was just ten feet away from me. The world needed a restart. As horrible as the bombs were, I've seen some great things come from them. You can always find some happiness in a shitty situation and that was it. Madison was able to rise as the world went into turmoil. This is what you three will be protecting. You will be protecting nature and the sense of community that the United States destroyed."

Omar, Natalie, and Jerrod tried to create a picture in their heads about what Grandpa just told them. They had a hard time creating this picture, as it was so unrealistic to them now. They believed Grandpa, though, and saw how upset he was while telling his story.

"Sorry I asked you to tell me that story Grandpa. I didn't mean to upset you," said Natalie as she rubbed his shoulder.

"No, it's good for you kids to know why you're fighting. I want all of you to fight so you'll never have to live like that again. Nature is where humans belong. Just like every other creature in this world. Humans are the only ones to overthink their existence and act more important than they really are. Be humble when you destroy the United States, because you'll need to teach them how to act once Madison is in charge." Grandpa said this proudly realizing these three were very promising to this world.

Tommy sat in his tent listening to everything Grandpa was saying. Tommy wanted to have fame. Grandpa spoke of murderers becoming famous and Tommy idolized that idea. Tommy loved the idea that people could know who he was by just doing the thing he loved to do the most, which was causing pain. Tommy wondered if maybe the United States was for him and that he was born into the wrong family.

Tommy laid his head on his pillow playing with the knife he had stolen from the digging exercise. He pictured being appreciated for his skills, unlike here, where Grandpa yelled at him all of the time.

The two weeks of training continued as Grandpa focused on cardio, shotgun drills, sniper rifle drills, pistol drills, assault rifle drills, and strength training.

Jerrod continued being the top shot with a sniper rifle. He was able to hit targets no other person in the Fairbanks family could imagine to hit. Natalie won every speed trial Grandpa put them through after the first day. Natalie also had the most accurate shooting, close range with the shotgun. Omar was not the fastest or the strongest, but he was the deadliest with the assault rifle. He hit his targets on point every time and was getting stronger day by day.

Tommy was the only one falling behind and unable to find a skill perfect for him. Most of the weapons were too heavy for him to hold properly for a long period of time. Grandpa was proud of Tommy nonetheless. He tried and did his best to keep up with his older friends.

"Well, you four survived the past two weeks of torture from me. I hope you'll still like me when we return to the cabin."

"I hope Grandma still likes you for being away for so long," said Omar.

"I really hope so, too. There's a good chance she forgot who I am though," said Grandpa.

Grandpa signaled all of the kids to lean in closer and had them take a knee near their now next-to-empty truck. The family had used most of the supplies they had brought for their trip.

"I'm so proud of all of you. You all completed this course and barely fought with me about the tasks you had to do. All four of you are going to make Madison proud one day. I'm confident you three will be respected by the Madison Army when you show up to their gates. And, Tommy, you did great this week, and I'm proud of you. You'll make a great Soldier one day, too. I'm sure of it."

Grandpa did his best to make Tommy feel a part of the team and wanted him to know he still loved him even if he acted distant and had a darker personality. Grandpa hoped these two weeks of family time dissolved the inner demons inside of the boy. Tommy did not have any moments that made Grandpa question him this week, which was reassuring.

The whole family hugged, even Tommy joined in on the family hug. He was hesitant at first but decided to embrace. They were all much closer than they had ever been. The Fairbanks family then entered the truck with Grandpa, Tommy, and Omar in the front. Jerrod and Natalie sat in the back together. The truck drove down the mountainside overlooking the woods.

Jerrod flexed his arm, asking Natalie to feel his muscle. Natalie gave a confidence-building smile. Natalie flexed her arm, and Jerrod made the same gestures to her. The two were exhausted and enjoyed sleeping on the soft seat in the truck compared to the rocky ground over the past two weeks. The two drifted off to sleep holding each other.

Omar, who was sitting in-between Grandpa and Tommy, fell asleep with his head tilted back in the air. Tommy was staring out of the window, day-dreaming as Grandpa drove the car. Grandpa continuously looked over at Tommy to check on him.

"I know you don't trust me, Grandpa, and I know you think I'm weird," said Tommy in the dead silent truck with only Grandpa awake.

"Tommy, I trust you."

"You don't even love me, and I know that."

"Tommy, you're my grandson. Of course I love you."

"No, you don't. You just do your best to tolerate me. You don't understand the kind of person I am, and you can't fix me because there's nothing wrong. This is who I am," said Tommy who felt extremely relieved to get this oral burden off his shoulders.

"You kill rats for fun, and that's who you are? You cut Omar and got a thrill from it, and that's just who you are?" asked Grandpa in a confused rage.

"Yes, Grandpa. I love killing and causing pain to things. I love it more than anyone in this truck. I get such a rush from slicing something open," said Tommy confidently knowing everyone was asleep and no one would believe Grandpa after having such a good two weeks with everyone else.

"What do I say to that, Tommy?"

"Nothing. I just want you to stop trying to change me, because it's a waste of time."

"You took my knife?"

"Yes, I did Grandpa, and I am keeping it. It is the perfect hook for tearing things and is a lot more brutal than just a straight edge scalpel."

Grandpa felt unsafe and was losing his mind that these words were coming out of the mouth of a fourteen-year-old boy.

"If you attack me, you'll look like the bad guy. So why don't you just stay out of my way, old man. If you don't, I'll have no trouble slitting your throat while you're sleeping next to Grandma."

Grandpa slammed on the breaks, causing everyone to fly forward, waking up everyone in the truck. He did not want to hear Tommy's craziness anymore.

He realized he just gave two weeks of weapon training to a psychotic fourteen-year-old. Grandma was wrong, and this was not a phase. He would be like this for as long as he lived. Grandpa did not know what route to take for action. Grandpa needed to let Jerrod know about his brother.

"Everything good, Grandpa?" asked Jerrod who awoke in a fright.

"Yeah, everything's fine. Just thought I saw a deer. Hey, Omar you mind staying up with me tonight to talk and keep me company?"

"Yeah, no problem, Grandpa," said Omar.

The truck continued driving into the night surrounded by woods, getting closer and closer to the Fairbanks cabin. Grandpa spent the entire trip planning what he would say to Jerrod about Tommy and what they should do. He did not feel safe sleeping in the same cabin with the maniac Tommy had revealed himself to be.

CHAPTER 11

Divided *May 10, 2046*

Nervousness about what was to come completely vanished from Marshall with his new life as an Elitist. Marshall had been properly trained on field signals and bomb planting skills over the past week.

Marshall laid in his bed staring at the ceiling with all of his gear and sniper rifle sitting at the side of the bed. It was completely quiet throughout the entire bunker. Marshall had no lights on in his room as he zoned out, planning all of the different situations that could happen. Tonight the team was splitting up into two squads and eliminating two cabins. Marshall would then follow Tar and Eros to Billings to plant the final bombs in the city. The other three members of the team would finally destroy the last cabin.

At that moment, Marshall would have one task left in the military. He would be overlooking the bombing at Billings, shooting any survivors and making sure that everything went smoothly.

Marshall would then be able leave the army with pride after finishing this mission and would be able to retire to West U.S. The only thought that kept bothering Marshall was the possibility of him feeling guilt after the bombing. Marshall's thoughts could not decide whether he would or not.

"Five minutes, Marshall," said Eros speaking through the closed door.

Marshall sat up on the bed, stared off one last time before entering war mode. Marshall looked at his bag, which contained explosives, his phone, food, water, and ammunition. Marshall threw the bag over his back, grabbed his sniper rifle, and headed for the door. Marshall entered the main room where he saw the other members checking their items to make sure that everything was to their satisfaction.

Eros walked out of his bedroom with his silenced assault rifle and a bag.

"Let's get going, ladies. Sorry, Nyx," said Eros with a sarcastic tone.

The team followed Eros up the ladder and back into the real world. The sun was completely set. The Elitists would be hidden by the night. All six members stood waiting for the final layout to tonight's mission and then everyone would head off to their respective tasks.

"Today's the big day, people. One of the last days of prep, and then we can finally see some fireworks. As I've been beating into your brains, all of you probably know the plan by heart now, but I'll give one last quick rundown. Marshall, Tar, and I will be executing the cabin closest to our current position, and then heading off to Billings to plant the final bombs. Ares, Nyx and Themis will be heading to the cabin just a little past the one we're attacking. You will camp there for at least two days picking off any wanderers that are trading shifts. After the two days are up, the three of you will head to the last cabin and destroy any inhabitants. We'll all regroup at the bunker after that's accomplished. Tar will then set off the explosions sending Marshall into retirement and the rest of us into the glorious memory of the U.S. history books."

"Yes, Sir," said the entire team to Eros.

"Let's get moving then," said Eros trying to pump up everyone.

Ares, Nyx, and Themis ran southwest to avoid the cabin Marshall's team would be attacking. Marshall, Eros, and Tar ran west to their target. This was Marshall's first cabin clearing, Marshall was ready to impress Eros, and reassure himself as a Soldier.

About an hour passed as Eros signaled to the team to slow down and crouch. Marshall slung his sniper rifle around to his hands and aimed down the sight toward the cabin.

"In sight?" asked Eros who questioned about the cabin.

Marshall did a scan of the area and spotted the two-story wood cabin.

"Down," said Marshall in a stern tone.

Eros and Tar both dropped to their stomachs, as trained to do. Marshall was hidden by a tree.

"They have a sniper sitting in the upper floor. They have one spotter but the two are just talking right now. They aren't even looking out the window."

The two-story cabin was surrounded by trees allowing an easy approach for intruders. Their sniper had less sight of enemies approaching. The same idea made Marshall's job a little more difficult but he was up for the challenge.

"According to the scout mission, there were only four people in this cabin. It's more of a family house. Two women and two men. The two men on the upper floor probably have a rifle by the window," said Eros.

"You're correct, Sir, the rifle seems to be just out of distance of the two," said Marshall.

"I know I am," smiled Eros.

Tar had been watching the area with binoculars giving the team extra eyes on the mission.

"Looks like they got a new dog," said Tar in a surprised voice.

Marshall aimed his rifle to the front porch where he saw a semi-large dog laying on the ground.

"Shoot the dog first then Tar and I will move up."

"Yes, Sir," said Marshall.

Marshall took aim at the dog who was asleep. Dogs could be the ultimate threat to a stealth team, because they are moving alarm systems that normally have a mean bite, too. Marshall relaxed his breathing and squeezed the trigger to his silenced sniper rifle. Tar watched the bullet strike the dog in the head.

"Confirmed hit," said Tar.

"Let's go get'em, Tar. Marshall keep an eye on the upper floor and vibrate me if they head downstairs," said Eros.

"Yes, Sir."

Tar and Eros walked through the heavily dense trees, doing their best to be as quiet as possible. The pair got to just thirty feet away from the front door of the cabin. The two men upstairs still had not moved or touched their rifle.

Eros signaled Tar to move behind the cabin, and he did just as he was told. Tar walked around the cabin keeping his thirty-foot difference between himself and the cabin. Tar noticed a woman outside working on a solar panel. Tar vibrated Eros phone signaling he had a clear shot and that she was alone. Eros vibrated back to Tar giving him the signal to kill.

Tar took aim at the woman who was staring down at her work. Tar fired one round of his silenced assault rifle. The round hit the woman directly in the chest causing her to fall backward away from the solar panel. This attack was not insight of Marshall due to the trees, so Marshall was unable to scout the surrounding area for Tar. Marshall did keep an eye on the two men upstairs who were still in the same place.

"Kill confirmed," read the message from Tar to Eros.

Tar continued his walk around the cabin, not noticing anything out of the ordinary or any threats. Eros had his gun aimed on the front door awaiting Tar's inspection of the area.

Marshall watched the entire area and saw another person head upstairs. There were now two men and one woman upstairs. Marshall passed this information to Eros through his phone.

Eros put Tar and Marshall into a group call and started speaking.

"Clearly these people have no idea what the hell's happening right now so we might as well talk this one out. I'm heading in the house. Marshall snipe the individual closest to the rifle. When I hear the rifle fired, I'll head up the stairs and kill the other two. These idiots will probably be looking the wrong way when I bust in. Wait for the vibrate and then shoot. Tar stay outside and look for wanderers. There shouldn't be any but play it safe."

"Yes, Sir," said Tar and Marshall at the same time.

Marshall took aim at the man who was closest to the rifle and now had the girl sitting on his lap. Marshall thought the three members inside the cabin could be no older than thirty. They were still a threat to the U.S. no matter what, and would kill the Elitists if given the chance. Marshall knew he needed to fire at them.

Eros snuck up on the porch in a hunched position, minimizing any sound. The door was unlocked. Eros let himself in and saw the staircase directly in front of him. Eros crept up the staircase, doing his best to make no noise.

Marshall had his scope on the man and woman sitting together. The woman was sitting on the man's lap. One shot should kill or at least immobilize them long enough for Eros to kill the others. Marshall received the vibration from his phone immediately causing him to shoot.

The shot could not be heard because it was silenced but it flew through the open window hitting the man in the chest and passing through to hit the women through her ribs. The woman fell off the chair, grasping her side trying to relieve the pain. The man sat in the chair while his head fell backward. His hands shook trying to cover his wound. The man sitting alone sat still with wide eyes trying to process what just happened, but by then it was too late.

Eros broke through the upstairs door, saw the man, and fired three assault rifle rounds into his chest, killing him instantly. Eros let go of his rifle, which was slung around him. Eros then grabbed his knife and chopped off the head of the man Marshall had shot. He threw the head to the woman on the ground who was now gasping for air. Fear engulfed her face as Eros approached her, closer and closer. He grabbed the top of her hair and smiled at her. Slowly, Eros stabbed the woman through the neck keeping a smile on his face throughout the entire experience. The woman's body went limp. Eros stood up from the dead woman's body and gave Marshall the all clear signal.

Marshall had to process what just happened. Marshall kept thinking to himself why Eros would kill her so slowly and why he had to smile while killing her? Maybe he was trying to scare future enemies, but no one was left alive to tell this story. Marshall was counting down the days until he would never have to see Eros again. Marshall walked to the cabin as Tar entered and dropped his bag to the ground. Tar prepped his explosives for this house. Eros walked down the stairs wiping his hands clean from the blood on the woman's shirt.

"Great shooting, Marshall. A two for one? Good work, Soldier."

"Thank you, Sir."

"I'm going to miss you when you're gone. You sure there's nothing I can do to get you to stay?"

"No, this will be my last mission," said Marshall with no hesitation in his voice.

"Well, just know the General will be missing you, Marshall."

"Thank you, Sir."

"You know that's pretty odd. General Quartz usually hates everyone, so congrats. I know you think I'm odd but if you were to stay and spend more time with him, you'd think that I'm the sanest person around," said Eros trying to bond with Marshall.

Marshall laughed and nodded to agree with Eros and then leaned down to help Tar out with the explosive set up.

"Hey, let Marshall set this one up. I mean we trained him so he may as well do some work," said Eros.

"I guess you're up to bat on this one," said Tar to Eros.

"I guess so."

Marshall unraveled the wire for the explosives. Eros left the room to have a phone call with Ares, informing him of the success. Tar turned to Marshall, as if he had been waiting to tell him something for some time.

"Do you actually not know what's going to be happening in a week and half from today?" asked Tar.

"The bombs will be going off."

"You're right, but that also starts the day of invasion. General Quartz is flying out to Billings with scientists and Soldiers and will be setting up around Billings."

"Why's he bringing scientists?"

"They're designing a missile launcher to attack Madison and the Canadians. This will end Madison. You seriously want to leave just before we end the war? You'll be forever remembered. The General will reward us with no end. My wife will have health care for life and you'll have a mansion by the coast. You seriously won't stick it out?"

Marshall stared at the ground continuing his work, while his mind rushed with concerns of what was right and what was wrong. Marshall weighed his thoughts. If he bombed Billings, he would be directly responsible for the death of millions. At the same time, if he bombed Billings, he would be a United States hero that would live on forever and he would have avenged his mother. Marshall continued to stare at the ground with his indecisiveness. Eros walked back into the room before Marshall could give an answer to Tar.

"This still isn't done yet? These take a second. Come on, let's get a move on it because the early bird gets the bomb planted," said Eros.

Marshall and Tar continued to work together in silence. Marshall had millions of thoughts running through his mind while Tar worried maybe he should not have told him the plan.

"Ares said they're attacking in two minutes. We're missing out on the fun," said Eros.

★ ★ ★

Ares looked down the scope to his silenced sniper rifle as Nyx, Themis, and he caught their breath.

"The cabin's in sight," said Ares to Nyx and Themis who were crouched behind him waiting on the forward signal.

"Which plan we using this time?" asked Nyx.

"Umm, how about we do something a little different. Marshall isn't here so let's have some fun with this cabin. I mean we only have this cabin and one more."

"What're you thinking?"

"Hand-to Hand-for you two only?" joked Ares.

"Challenge accepted," said Nyx while laughing.

Themis chuckled, too, once Nyx started to laugh. The two met eyes and knew they were capable of executing this challenge.

"As long as you're as good of a shot as Marshall," said Nyx to Ares.

Ares's face immediately went straight as he glared at Nyx in anger.

"Relax, dick, it was just a joke."

Themis nodded his head as Nyx spoke.

"Well, you two think you're so good, why don't you just go in hand-to-hand then?" asked Ares with anger growing within his tone.

"Fine. Just get the wanderers that come and go. Themis and I will kill everyone in the cabin. You get everyone outside."

"Deal."

Nyx pulled out a map of the area from her bag. The map was a zoomed-in image of this cabin specifically. There were notes on the side of the map describing the scout's mission taken previously.

"All right, there should be four Soldiers in the cabin sleeping right now. There should be four Soldiers walking around in the area. Finally, if we look at how frequent they trade Soldiers in and out, we'll see that tomorrow afternoon, there's likely to be a trade. Then we destroy the last cabin."

Ares did not like being told what to do by anyone who was not a superior. He stared at Nyx with anger throughout her entire speech.

"We obviously know that, Nyx. Let's just get a move on it or you worried they're going to kick your ass in that cabin?"

Nyx stood from her crouched position and packed her things. She walked toward Ares and signaled Themis to follow.

"Just don't make me regret not asking Marshall to come with us instead," said Nyx as she passed him.

Ares pushed Nyx from behind as she walked past him, causing her to stumble forward. Themis immediately grabbed Ares shirt with both hands and pushed him at full speed toward a tree. Ares was unable to get his arms up to defend himself, as Themis's elbows were outstretched to block any chance of Ares doing anything.

"Just so you know, I could kick your ass, Ares, so don't let Themis fool you. I am the deadly one of the family. Let's go, Themis."

Themis let go of Ares, allowing his body to unclench and slide down from the tree. Ares's face of fear and shock disappeared and turned into an arrogant smile.

"Only one more week with the bitch and the retard," said Ares not loud enough to be heard by Nyx and Themis.

Ares grabbed his dropped bag and rifle from the ground. Ares ran toward a more advantageous position for the attack to come. Just like many missions before, this was a solo, one-story cabin in the middle of woods created by hunters but now inhabited by Madisons and Canadians.

This cabin did not have any defined pathways, which would make this mission trickier as Ares did not know where the enemy would be emerging. Ares went to his bag, grabbed tree stakes, and started to stab them into a tree that overlooked the cabin. Ares was able to help Nyx and Themis if needed but still snipe any wanderers.

Nyx and Themis laid flat on the ground next to the last tree by the porch of the cabin. The cabin seemed to have one main room with two bedrooms. The porch had a wooden overhang, which seemed to be the only main difference between this cabin and others.

"Remember Themis, only knives and hand-to-hand."

Themis nodded and looked on toward the cabin with determination. Ares sent a message to Nyx who felt the vibration.

"None spotted," read the message from Ares.

"Ares has no sign of the wanderers, but let's just get our share done," said Nyx to Themis.

There were no signs of light in the cabin or any signs of anyone being awake, which was not surprising with the time of night.

"Let's do this," said Nyx.

The two removed some gear so they would be faster at hand-to-hand, and they left their assault rifles on the ground. Nyx and Themis only held a 6" combat knife with built in brass knuckles. The two approached the door slowly and stealthily. No signs of life were to be found as they continued forward. Nyx slowly opened the door, took one-step in the door, and made eye contact with a Soldier who had a machine gun aimed at the door. Themis threw Nyx backward to avoid the gunfire as Themis dove to the right to save himself, too.

Shots fired, as the front of the cabin became riddled with bullet holes. Ares took aim at the cabin but had no clear shots of the enemy. Nyx was on the ground covering her head and crawling closer to Themis who was safely hidden to the side of the house. The shots stopped firing as three Soldiers ran out, all with machine guns pointing in different directions.

Ares took aim and shot as soon as the three men walked outside of the cabin. The bullet went through one Soldier's neck and through the chest of the man behind him. The third Soldier turned his gun toward Ares direction and randomly fired his gun towards the trees.

Themis reached around from the side of the cabin and pulled the Soldier backward onto his back using the Soldier's collar. Themis's giant arms held the Soldier's gun tightly so the Soldier could not fire at Themis. Themis continued holding the man's gun and with his left hand, pulled out his knife, and stabbed the man upwards from his throat into his skull.

Another two Soldiers ran out the door with one getting sniped in the back by Ares. The other Soldier took aim at Themis, who was now around the side of the house and safe from Ares. As he took aim, Nyx threw her knife at the Soldier, landing in the center of his chest. The Soldier stumbled backward while getting hit and Themis grabbed the Soldier by the ankle and took his feet out from underneath him. Themis stabbed the Soldier the same way he did the last. He ripped out Nyx's knife and handed it back to her. The two ran toward the tree line to regroup.

There were only three Soldiers left inside the cabin if their scout mission was correct and there were only teams of eight. Ares kept his scope on the surrounding area searching for any slight movement. There were no signs of movement. Anyone left inside the cabin was set on staying in there. Ares checked his back to make sure no one had spotted his position from his shooting. Ares felt safe and continued scoping out the area.

Nyx and Themis crawled through the woods in hopes of not getting caught. They were both only armed with their knives because they failed to pick up any of the weapons dropped by the enemy.

"You think we can still do this with just hand-to-hand?" asked Nyx with a smirk on her face.

Themis nodded his head with a giant smirk on his face. Nyx jumped up into a crouched position looking through the woods, checking for enemies, and checking back at the cabin. She saw the tip of a gun pop out through a window.

The Soldier inside the cabin could not see Nyx but was searching the area. Nyx saw the gun fall to the ground and the man yelled as he backed away from the window. Ares had landed a shot on the Soldier's weapon.

Nyx went to her phone, which was attached to her wrist as they were made to work this way. She typed a message to Ares.

"Fire bird," read the message.

Ares aimed his rifle down for a moment while he looked in his bag and searched for a flash bang bullet. When the bullet hit a target, a bright light was triggered, temporarily blinding and disorientating anyone within a twenty-foot radius.

Ares received another message and checked his phone.

"Still counts as just hands," read the message from Nyx.

Ares smiled while loading the round into his sniper rifle. Ares took aim at the cabin and waited for Nyx to signal when she was moving toward the cabin.

Nyx and Themis, who were still crouched and undiscovered by the troops in the cabin, stood in the tree line deciding the best plan of attack.

"I'm guessing the machine gun is still aimed at the front door so I want you to throw a rock into the cabin to see how trigger happy these people are. I'll be in the back of cabin and jump in through the window. You hold the front once the flash goes off."

Themis nodded and waited as Nyx walked through the woods to reach the back of the cabin.

Nyx vibrated Themis's phone, which signaled him to throw a rock at the cabin. Themis had found a baseball sized rock and hurled it into the cabin. The machine gun fired into the woods in front of the cabin. Themis was clear of any bullets and snuck his way to the porch.

Ares received a vibration and fired the fire bird into the cabin. A large bright light filled the cabin, blinding the Soldiers inside the cabin. One man screamed as his eyes burned from the light.

Nyx was up next. She broke the window in the back of the cabin with her brass knuckles and jumped inside the cabin. A Soldier was facing her with a rifle and tried to fire but was out of ammo. The Soldier's arm covered his face as blood was dripping from his eyes. Nyx had her knife in her right hand, rushed toward the man, and stabbed the Soldier in the stomach four times rapidly. She then pulled the man's arm away from his face and punched him with her brass knuckles. The man fell limp to the ground and Nyx ran toward her next target.

The Soldier using the machine gun, faced the front of the cabin, but was sitting on his butt with both of his hands on his face, crying, as if he took a direct hit from the fire bird. His eyes bled and his screams continued. Nyx ran up behind him, pulled his head up by his hair, and stabbed him through the neck with one quick motion, ending his screams and causing him to drop to his back.

The last Soldier was standing in the front corner of the cabin. His pistol was drawn. He seemed to have been the least affected by the fire bird. He took aim at Nyx, who ran toward him.

Nyx started losing confidence and time slowed down; worried she was not quick enough. This house clearing was no more than thirty seconds long, but maybe that was still just a second too much.

Just before the Soldier took his shot at Nyx, Themis's hand came through the window grabbing the Soldier's right hand, which was holding the gun, and Themis slammed the Soldier's arm against the wall, squeezing with all of his might. The gun fell from his hand and Themis pulled the Soldier out of the cabin by his arm. Themis threw him to the ground outside on the dirt just before the tree line.

Themis looked back to Nyx to see if she was okay. Nyx gave him a nod with a smile, and Themis returned the gesture. Themis then looked forward toward the Soldier laying on the ground, clenching his now broken arm with blood shot eyes.

Themis walked toward the man and threw his knife on the ground between them. Themis looked at him and pointed toward the knife. Themis proceeded to put his hands up in a boxing motion, signaling a fight.

The Soldier had confidence now that the knife was in front of him. He stood up, rushed toward the knife, picked it up with his unbroken arm, and charged Themis with the knife outstretched in front of him. Themis swiped the knife away with his right hand and proceeded with an inhumanly strong left hook, knocking the man to the ground. The knife fell from his hand and blood squirted from his lip. He laid flat on his stomach.

Ares had his sniper rifle on the fight the entire time to make sure nothing went wrong. Nyx finished searching the cabin for troops. The cabin was clear, so she headed outside to watch the end of the fight.

Themis looked toward Nyx and Ares who were watching his fight. Themis enjoyed the attention he was receiving. Themis straddled the man's back who was still conscious. Themis put his fingers underneath the man's jaw looking for a good grip. Themis pulled upward trying to rip the man's head off from his body. The screams were more horrendous than the screams from the fire bird. Themis's plan was not working as expected. Themis let go of his head and grabbed his knife, which was on the ground near him. He sawed off half of the Soldier's head while the Soldier screamed horrifically. All the noise ended abruptly. Themis cleanly pulled off the Soldier's head.

Themis let out a large grunt and held the man's head in the air.

"Thank you, Themis, for saving me in there."

Themis dropped the head to the ground and acknowledged Nyx with a nod. Ares was already packed up and walking over to Nyx and Themis.

"Good work you two." said Ares.

"Let's set up the trip wire and head to the trees. We'll watch for the next day or so and head to the last cabin. Recon says there're only six people in this cabin and Tar checked this place out just a month ago. It should be a quick cabin and then we can head back to base and wait for the last mission," said Ares.

"Sounds good, Ares. Just let Eros know we're clear," said Nyx.

"Right."

Ares walked away for a second and sent a message to Eros.

"Cabin clear. Campout begins," read the message.

CHAPTER 12

Implant   *May 10, 2046*

Bombs were a lot smaller than one would think. Marshall, Tar, and Eros each had five bombs in their bags. They had fifteen different locations to plant their bombs. Eros already had an idea and mapped out the few buildings left that needed to be planted. The three of them entered the city of Billings from the tree line.

"Ahh, we're home now," said Eros sarcastically while stretching.

"Where're we heading, Sir?" asked Marshall.

"Well, there's a bar in town that still needs planting, and then the hotel is the last target that needs to be planted. Tonight we'll get the bar and then check-in to the hotel in the morning."

The three continued walking toward the bar, which was actually quite full of people at this time. They all got something to drink and relaxed for about an hour.

"Ares said they finished their job," said Eros looking up from his phone.

"Cheers to them," said Tar in a tipsy excitement.

"They only have one cabin left and then this phase of the mission will finally be behind us," said Eros happily.

Marshall did not say much as his nerves kicked in with everything that was going on. He worried about what he would be forced to do soon. Marshall continued drinking with Eros with Tar by his side, knowing with every little task he was forced to do, he was one-step closer to being retired.

"Marshall, why don't you head to the bathroom and take care of some business for me since you don't seem to be enjoying our company," said Eros.

Marshall happily walked away from their pointless small talk. Marshall grabbed his bag and headed toward the bathroom. Tar had shown him several times over the past week about how to set up these bombs. The bombs themselves where just about the size of a half-gallon of milk. There was a wireless receiver in the bomb that triggered the explosion when Eros's phone gave the signal. It was rectangular and solid black. Not too much show to this item but it packed an aggressive punch.

Marshall entered the bathroom and to his luck, it was empty. There were about twenty people in the bar itself, but none in the men's bathroom. Marshall went to one of the stalls and locked the door. He put the bag of bombs on the top of the toilet and grabbed one of the bombs. There were no buttons or anything on these bombs. All Marshall had to do was place it in the correct location and turn it to the right frequency with his phone. Marshall linked the phone to the bomb and set the bomb to the right frequency code. All was set and Marshall moved to the next step.

The ceiling tile was the same as most buildings in the city. Marshall lifted the tile and placed the bomb on top of the tile. He let the tile down to its original position, left the bathroom with his bag, and sat down with Tar and Eros at the bar again.

"Everything come out all right?" asked Eros.

"Very smooth," said Marshall.

"Oh my goodness, did you just tell a joke?" asked Eros surprisingly.

Marshall smiled and put his drink in the air toward Eros and began to drink. Marshall felt he might as well put up a good front toward Eros. Marshall knew he would only need to see him for one more week and should do his best to stay on his good side.

The three of them continued to drink through the night until sunrise at which point the team would head to the hotel to check-in. Eros received a tap on his shoulder just as the team was about to leave. It was Julie from the restaurant.

"Hey, you're back in town," said Julie with excitement.

Eros smiled and signaled her for a hug, and Eros kissed her on the cheek.

"What're you up to tomorrow? You want to meet up for a little?" asked Julie to Eros.

"I'd love that. My friends and I are staying at the hotel, and we're booking a room in the morning. I'd love if you stopped by."

"I would love to," said Julie in a flirtatious manner.

"Don't you have to work at Tina's?" asked Eros.

"I took the next week off for vacation. I have family in Canada expecting me the day after tomorrow," said Julie excitedly and now seeming to be drunk.

"Well, I'll see you around noon tomorrow?"

"That seems kind of early, but I guess that can work."

The two kissed, hugged, and said their goodbyes as Eros, Tar, and Marshall started walking away.

"Aren't we sharing a room? I don't want to see you bang that girl," said Tar.

"Don't worry, you two will be planting bombs at noon, and I'll be dealing with her on my own."

The team entered the lobby of the six-story hotel and were greeted by a man at the front desk.

"Welcome to Last Hotel Inn," said the deskman.

"Thanks, I'd like one room for the three of us. It's about to get real messy up there so I suggest you have some maids on standby," said Eros. The deskman did not understand and awkwardly smiled. Marshall and Tar felt awkward, too. The two walked toward the stairs to wait for Eros.

"Well, I thought it was funny but just one room please. Only one night, too."

The deskman started filling out some paperwork by hand and gave Eros a copy with a key.

"Just return the key when you're done and have a nice stay."

"Thank you very much and you, too," said Eros, who walked away toward the stairs where Tar and Marshall waited.

"Top floor, guys," yelled Eros in a still tipsy excitement.

The team walked up the flights of stairs to the top of the building. They opened the door to their room, saw two twin beds, and a small bathroom.

"Wow, what a shit hole," said Eros who looked around the room.

"I've seen worst," said Tar.

"All right, well let's take a nice four or so hours rest and then get ready to work."

Eros and Tar grabbed a bed each for themselves while Marshall set up a make shift bed on the ground. It was not the coziest place to sleep but anything was better than sleeping on the ground in the woods.

Marshall had trouble falling asleep. He had anxiety, just wanted to finish this mission, and wanted to stop sleeping in enemy territory. Eros was able to separate times of threat and times of relaxation extremely well. Marshall did not have this ability. Marshall only felt safe in the bunker and was on edge anytime out of the bunker. Tar seemed to fall asleep fast, too, which meant he might have been dead tired or drunk. Marshall thought to himself about how weird it was that Eros had a date with a woman the same day that they were planting fourteen bombs in this building.

Marshall stared out the window of their sixth floor room and heard Eros's phone alarm ring.

Eros got out of bed and saw Marshall was not sleeping.

"I'm beginning to think you're a robot, my friend," said Eros to Marshall.

"Just ready to do the mission, Sir."

"Well, wake up Tar. Both of you split up the rooms and head out. Each of you plant one bomb on each floor in different rooms making sure they're hidden away. I'll plant a few on this floor but first I have a quick date with Julie."

Marshall woke Tar while Eros headed to the bathroom.

"Let's get moving, man."

"All right, I'm up," said Tar in a drained and sleepy voice.

Marshall and Tar grabbed their bags and headed to the fifth floor. Inside their bags was a special fit key that adjusted to fit the lock for every specific lock. The key grew or shrunk certain parts to fit the key hole perfectly.

Each were to plant bombs in one room, different from each other's on each floor. There were eight rooms on each floor and the hotel was far from being filled at this time of day. It would be simple to have two bombs per floor.

Eros looked at himself in the mirror one last time and headed down to the first floor where the lobby was and most likely Julie.

Eros walked down the staircase and entered the lobby, which had eight rooms as well and the front desk. There stood Julie, looking better than ever without her work uniform.

"You found the place!"

"Of course, I did," laughed Julie.

"Well, why don't we head up to my room and relax a little, since we've both been out most of the night."

"Sounds good to me."

The two began walking together up the stairs, heading to his room. Neither were talking. Julie started feeling uncomfortable so she created some small talk.

"So do you live around here since you're here every once in a while?"

"Yeah, I have a cabin just south of Billings with some of my friends. My dad passed away and told me that I could have the cabin, so I left Madison and headed up here with some of my friends. The rustic life is a lot better than the city life, but I need a dose of city from time to time."

"Yeah, I understand. This place is kind of small from where I'm from actually."

"You said you were from Canada, right?"

"Yeah, there's a very populated city just between the old U.S. and Canadian border north of here. They actually supply this city quite a bit. That's how I got a job down here."

Eros thought to himself and became irritated that there were so many survivors in the north from the bombings years ago. Most of North America was saved due to the Navy in the Pacific, but many Canadian cities were hit as the Navy focused their targets on just U.S. striking missiles. Unfortunately, for Eros and his team, it seemed many southern Canadian cities stayed quiet during the U.S. Civil War and now are thriving.

Eros did not speak or acknowledge Julie the rest of the walk up the stairs.

The two got to the room and Eros unlocked the door, looked toward Julie, and signaled her forward. Julie smiled and entered but felt nervous as her friends thought she left for Canada and no one knew she was at the hotel.

Eros shut the door behind him and turned the lock.

"That's a nice view you got there," said Julie trying to ease the tension.

"I have a very nice view in front of me right now."

Julie smiled and began to relax a little. Eros approached her slowly and looked down to her as he went in for a kiss. Julie kissed him back passionately. Eros squatted down, grabbed Julie by the legs, and picked her up in the air while kissing her. Julie was blown away with romance and only thought about how attractive Eros was.

Eros started to become more aggressive with the kissing and tossed her onto the bed fiercely. Julie was surprised but still enjoyed everything that was happening. Eros slowly went in for a kiss with Julie, now laying on the bed. Julie closed her eyes anticipating a kiss but was smacked in the face by Eros with his full strength. She wanted to scream but now Eros was on top of her putting all of his weight onto his forearm, which pressed on her throat. Julie had trouble breathing and panicked but no noise came out of her. Eros began making out with Julie who was unable to breathe and about to faint.

Julie blacked out and Eros took his pressure off her throat so as not to kill her. Eros ran over to his bag and grabbed zip ties to bind Julie because he had dozens of ideas of what to do with a Canadian Outlier.

Meanwhile, Marshall and Tar planted bombs throughout the hotel. Marshall was now on the first floor and was trying to be stealthy. All rooms were occupied on the first floor so Marshall figured the janitor's closet would be a good choice to plant this bomb.

Tar handed Marshall one of his bombs and Marshall headed to the closet. Tar walked up to the room to make sure Eros was planting his bombs and not completely wasting the mission's time.

Marshall looked around and saw the front deskman sitting down, reading a book. Marshall saw this was a good time to head to the janitor's closet. Marshall made his move and shut the closet door behind him. Marshall turned on a light switch. The room itself was rather small and was one room with a rack of tools in the center and tons of equipment and cleaning supplies on the walls.

Marshall noticed the ceiling in there was solid and he could not plant the bomb like he had been doing. Marshall figured he could hide the bomb behind or in an empty cleaning supply bucket. Marshall looked for a bucket in the back of the room and found exactly what he needed. It was a stack of mop buckets, which went from the ground to the ceiling. Marshall figured he could plant two bombs in the buckets that were toward the center of the stack that no one would use or find within the next week.

Marshall took the buckets apart but then heard the door open behind him.

"What're you doing in here?" asked the janitor.

Marshall turned around to see it was an older man in janitorial clothing with a pistol drawn.

"I just needed a bucket because I made a mess in my room."

Marshall's hands were in the air signaling he was not a threat to the janitor. Marshall slowly walked toward the janitor with his hands in the air.

"Hey, stop moving. You know you're trespassing," yelled the janitor.

"I'm sorry. I just needed a bucket. I can go now," said Marshall who stopped moving but kept his hands in the air.

"Fine. Get out before I shoot your ungrateful ass."

Marshall put his hands down, grabbed the bag with two bombs left in it, and put it around his back.

"Give me your bag," said the janitor.

"Why?"

"Because I make the money you would think a janitor would make so give me the fucking bag and go on your way or get shot for trespassing. Then I'll keep all of your stuff anyway. Your choice."

Marshall threw his bag toward the janitor's feet and started walking toward the door while the janitor had his gun still drawn. Marshall watched the janitor's eyes and waited for the perfect moment to make a move. Just as he was almost out the door, he noticed the janitor looked down at the bag for a second. Marshall drew his silenced pistol and shot the janitor in the center of his forehead. The janitor fell to the ground and bled-out. Marshall went to grab the janitor's pistol and realized it was unloaded. Marshall laughed to himself but continued to plant the bombs in the buckets.

Marshall finished planting the bombs and grabbed a garbage bag to cover the janitor from being found. After the janitor was in the garbage bag, Marshall jammed the dead man into a locker that was in the room. Marshall did his best to clean up the blood but figured no one would pay too much attention to the mess. Marshall was done planting bombs for this mission and headed back to their room to meet with the team.

Marshall got to the sixth floor and saw Tar sitting in the hallway.

"What's going on?" asked Marshall.

"He must be banging her good or something."

Marshall sat down next to Tar in the hallway and waited to be let back into the room.

"So you're really leaving, huh?" asked Tar.

"Yeah, after next week I will officially be retired from the army."

"What happened? You were chosen because you kill mercilessly and now you have a conscience for this stuff?"

"I can kill a man who threatens me or my fellow citizen but I was finding it hard to connect the killing of the people in this city to eliminating threats. I mean I understand and I don't at the same time. I get bad people emerge from Madison but not everyone here will try to kill me. On the other hand, though, it's the exact opposite. Any person from Madison could one day be a threat. This is why I'm confused and find this mission hard to carry out. But I promised the General and the U.S. that I'd carry out this mission and that's what I'll do even if I second guess every single action I make."

"I get it. I had some trouble at first, too, but then I put my wife's needs in front of my own and that's why I'm staying on as long as they need me."

"Does your wife know what you do over the wall to pay for her bills?"

"No."

"I think if she did, she would tell you to stop. We'll be remembered for this mission. The stories will tell how we destroyed armies of Soldiers in Billings when in reality we killed thousands of unarmed people at a local pub. The war stories are created by the people in charge and citizens will listen blindly. We'll know what really happened but if we speak up, we'll be killed."

Tar sat there taking in everything Marshall just said, realizing he was right. Marshall spoke again to finalize his point to Tar about why he was confused.

"Prior to leaving that wall, I was blind to how society ran. But the second I saw a family begging me to take their kid. I knew the U.S. wasn't a good country. They were just really good at telling news the way they want it to be seen. That's what changed me, and why I'm not as merciless as Eros wanted me to be. This is why this's my last mission, because I want to make my mother proud, but at the same time, I need to sleep at night."

"I get it, I do. When the bombs go off I think I'll request some time off to see my wife so I can get some encouragement for what I'm fighting for again."

"Feel free to head to West U.S. with your wife on your leave."

The two continued to talk and discuss their feelings and ideas toward the plans that were nearing. Just a doorway away Eros had Julie tied to the bed with her mouth taped shut.

"Oh good, you're awake. Why do you look so scared? The worst is over now, Julie. You already swallowed the pill."

"As you are probably guessing at this point, I'm from the States. Wow that felt amazing to say out loud to you. I mean it feels so good to tell someone you love the truth," Eros continued speaking and pacing around the room like a crazy person.

"Oh no, this is no way to tell someone you love them. Pretend you heard nothing. No, wait, I have a better idea."

Eros grabbed the knife from his side and mounted Julie who was now terrified. Eros sliced off her right ear and threw it on the bed.

"Now you'll never know that I said I love you," said Eros whispering into her left ear.

Julie's screams were muffled and unable to be heard.

"I hate Canadians, and I hate Madisons. You're a crossbreed shit of both, and that's why I felt so dirty when you told me those things. So, naturally, I had to cleanse myself and what better way than to just let you dissolve. Remember how I told you that you swallowed that pill? Well, that pill is a beautiful torture tool used by the U.S. It'll make your stomach acids extra acidic. The change in acidity will melt your stomach lining, causing the acid to melt your innards."

Julie was now horrified. Eros said everything with a grand smile on his face and continued sitting on top of her, as she was spread on the bed and unable to move.

"You'll experience pain for about ten minutes but after that point, your stomach will have been destroyed and there's nothing I can do for you. The really funny part of all of this is that you only need a glass of water to cancel out this chemical process," said Eros with a laugh.

"Unfortunately for you, your mouth is taped shut, and I can't get any water down your mouth."

Julie felt the pain that Eros talked about and started squirming in discomfort.

"Ahh, I see the pill has begun the dissolve process. I don't need to pry any information from you, so I'll just get a joy from watching you squirm over the next ten minutes."

Julie laid there for five minutes, as the pain continued to increase with every minute. Eros still sat on her causing more discomfort.

"Oh, look! A glass of water! Your one true savior. Here let me help."

Eros poured water over Julie's face but no water could be swallowed because her mouth was taped shut.

"Come on, silly. Open wide."

The ten-minute mark arrived and there was no saving Julie. The acid melted through many of her organs and blood started coming out of her nose. Eros cut the ties that had her bound. She tried to attack him but was too weak. The more she moved, the more pain she experienced.

"All right, let's go, pretty thing," said Eros as he picked her up and threw her over his shoulder as she screamed through the tape.

Eros carried her to the bathroom and chucked her into the bathtub.

"The next part is pretty gross and I don't want you messing up the bed any more than you already have. I guess this is goodbye, my beautiful lady friend."

Eros leaned in for a kiss and kissed her taped mouth. Her hands were too weak to stop him or pull the tape off her mouth. She laid in the tub slowly drifting off to her death.

Eros cleaned up the bloodstain from the bed from when he cutoff her ear. Eros grabbed the ear from the bed and threw it in the bathtub with Julie.

Eros walked to the door to his room, unlocked it, and let Tar and Marshall into the room.

"What's that smell?" asked Tar.

"Julie doesn't know how to handle herself and I'm pretty sure she shit herself, too," said Eros in a joking tone.

The door to the bathroom was open and Marshall saw Julie's lifeless body in the bathtub. Marshall ran over to her, removed the tape from her mouth, and blood pooled out form her mouth. Julie was dead. Her back was completely dissolved, with blood and semi-dissolved organs falling into the bathtub.

"What the fuck are you doing?" shouted Marshall with rage as he ran out of the bathroom to get into Eros's face.

"Stand down, Soldier. I'm in charge, and she was a threat, so I made a judgment call. Kill her now or kill her in the explosion. It shouldn't make a difference to you, Marshall. Now did you plant the bombs?"

Marshall stared into the bathroom, having never seen such a disfigured person. Tar spoke up for Marshall.

"Yes, all floors are set, Sir."

"Very good, Soldier. If you'd please set up my bombs for me on this floor while I clean up my mess," said Eros.

Marshall gave one last look of anger toward Eros but then started walking. Eros responded with a large smile to push Marshall's buttons even more.

"Oh, wait before you go, just wanted you both to know. Ares scouted out the last cabin and only one person is inhabiting it so they figured they would speed up the cabin attacks and get it done tomorrow morning. Just wanted you both to be in the loop. Plant those bombs and then we can head back to the bunker tomorrow night and finalize our plans for the attack," said Eros trying to motivate Marshall and get his head back in the game for what they were doing here. Eros knew Marshall would not understand what happened to Julie so there was no need to try to explain it to him.

Marshall and Tar nodded and headed out to set up the bombs. Tar would plant a bomb in this room tomorrow night right before they left for the bunker.

Marshall and Tar left the room as Eros went to the bathroom and locked the door. Julie was completely bled-out, which would make hiding her body much easier. Eros started to cut her body into pieces to fit into the small trash bags the room provided him. The body was now in ten pieces and squeezed into a few garbage bags. Eros threw the bags into the ceiling through tiles he could lift. He knew no one would be looking there because no one would assume there would be a body in the ceiling. By the time the smell drifts into the room, the hotel would be in ruins.

Eros was pleased with his work as the leader of this mission. He headed back to his bed and laid down enjoying the last few hours he spent with Julie. Tar and Marshall entered the room to see Eros in bed.

"Everything is set, Sir," said Marshall in a pissed-off tone.

"Fantastic. Well, we just need to wait for Ares's team to take out the last cabin and remove any wandering threats to their current cabin. We'll stay until tomorrow looking for places we could have missed with bombs and places that will be good to camp while we watch over the explosions."

Marshall and Tar nodded their heads and both sat down trying to process what they had seen earlier. This was yet another time Marshall was counting down the time left under the control of the crazy Eros.

CHAPTER 13

The Fairbanks *May 12, 2046*

Grandma woke up in her big bed, which had been emptier than normal. She reached for her husband, but he was nowhere to be found. She had no one to make the coffee so she knew her day would have to begin earlier than normal yet again, now that the family had been gone for a few days.

Grandma walked downstairs holding the railing with all of her might as her leg continued to worsen day-by-day. She started the coffee machine, which had enough energy left in it from the prior day's solar panel charge. The coffee brewed while Grandma walked over to Grandpa's chair. She put her head back and tried to relax.

As she was sitting there with her eyes shut and mind at ease, she heard a scratching noise. It did not seem to be anywhere in her direct area but she wondered if it was from upstairs. It was not an unusual occurrence since they lived in the woods and rodents would get inside every occasionally. Grandma wanted to find the animal so it did not have babies and nest. With all of her strength, Grandma got up from the chair, trying to put minimum weight on her bad leg, and started her journey upstairs to investigate the noise.

Grandma took a break halfway up the stairs to rest her leg and listen for any noises. She heard more scratching coming from Omar and Tommy's room. Grandma reached for the door, now that she made it up the stairs, and heard the scratching more clearly now. Grandma opened the door slowly and a small mouse ran out through the door. It was fast so Grandma did not see where the mouse ran.

Grandma looked at the ground in search of the mouse but was unable to find anything. To her surprise, she found mouse footprints in an off-shade of red, leading to Tommy's closet. It was a bloody foot print trail from the mouse. This grabbed her attention. She was now extremely curious as to why the mouse was bloody. Grandma walked over to the closet and opened the door. There was a floor panel with a corner chewed away, which she assumed was where the mouse originated.

Grandma slowly went to her knees trying not to put herself in any pain. She lifted the wood piece and screamed in shock. There were dozens of decapitated mice laying in a box underneath the floorboard. Grandma felt sick as she looked closer to see that some still had their heads attached but all of their limbs were missing. The mouse she saw must have gotten away or Tommy just did not have enough time to kill it yet.

Grandma rested her head on the wall in the closet while thousands of worries entered her mind. She knew Grandpa was right the whole time, and that Tommy had some inner demons that needed to be expressed. This was not just a phase anymore; this was who Tommy was. Tommy was a kid that enjoyed causing pain to others. There were so many signs, but only Grandpa was able to identify and realize the problem.

Grandma thought of ways to let her family, in the mountains, know to keep their distance from Tommy until she could create a plan. She cried and wanted her husband here to comfort her. That was not a choice right now, though, and she was aware. Grandma thought to herself that there was nothing she could do right this second, so there was no need to worry about Tommy.

Grandma pulled herself up from the floor in Tommy's closet and covered the hole with the floorboard. She walked downstairs to find her coffee was done brewing. She poured herself a cup and sat in Grandpa's chair, wishing he were here so they could talk to Tommy together.

"Spotted," whispered Ares to Nyx and Themis who were crouching near him at the base of a tree just fifty yards away from the Fairbank's cabin.

"Just one person, just like yesterday."

"Ok. Shoot the door open, and I'll rush in for the kill. She doesn't seem to be too mobile, right?" asked Nyx.

"Not at all," laughed Ares.

"Vibrate when you're ready to move in," said Ares.

Themis and Nyx approached the cabin slowly and steadily. It was morning and the sun was shining down on the team. The sooner this was done, the sooner they could head back to the bunker to prep for the final explosion. Nyx and Themis were extremely lucky for not walking into one of the traps set by the Fairbanks. The two did not even notice they existed but managed to avoid all of them without even trying. The traps were perfectly camouflaged.

Nyx was now at the end of the tree line laying on her stomach, just forty feet away from the front of the cabin.

"Themis stay here this time while I head in. No need for both of us for just this one old hag," laughed Nyx.

Nyx hopped into a crouched position readying herself to run forward as the door was blown open by the sniper rifle shot. Ares had his scope locked on the door. Nyx sent the vibration and ran toward the door. Ares immediately fired on the door, blowing open the door. Nyx was almost inside as the door flew from the hinges.

The door blowing open turned on Grandma's adrenaline as she grabbed the sawed off shotgun lodged in-between the cushion of Grandpa's chair. She then immediately fell to the floor to minimize the enemy's target of her. Nyx ran inside to surprisingly see Grandma in a prone position aiming down the sights of her shotgun and firing away. The spread shot hit Nyx in the left shoulder wounding her, causing her to collapse and return out the front door. Nyx angrily signaled she needed help. Themis immediately ran toward Nyx as Ares looked for a clean shot at Grandma.

Grandma crawled forward to Grandpa's chair and reached under the chair to find more shotgun shells. Grandma reloaded the gun while her back was against the chair, which was not facing the front door. Grandma reloaded the gun but felt that someone was watching her. She turned around to see Themis standing over her and the chair with a giant grin on his giant face. Grandma turned to fire a shot at Themis, but Themis kicked the chair forward causing Grandma to miss her shot, knocking her forward with an empty gun. Themis threw the chair out of the way, grabbed Grandma by her foot, and dragged her closer to him. He spun her around so she was facing up and looking directly at Themis.

"Oh, just kill me if you're going to do it, you big pansy," yelled Grandma.

Themis's smile faded and his grip tightened on Grandma's leg. Themis grabbed his silenced pistol from his side and shot Grandma in the chest three times. Grandma began to drift away as she reached for Grandpa's turned over chair near her. Themis saw her arm move and fired one more shot into her head, killing her. Themis vibrated Ares signaling it was all clear.

Ares packed up his area and ran toward the cabin.

"You got defeated by a little old lady?" yelled by an overjoyed Ares.

"It's just a scrape and the dumb bitch is dead now, so technically I won," said Nyx.

"Let me patch it up for you before we plant this bomb and head back."

"Fuck this cabin. This is the last one and I've been shot so let's put the weight triggered one in. Whoever else lives here deserves a painful death. Forget the tripwire. We blew the door open anyway so they'll notice by the time they get to the front."

"This is our last cabin so we might as well go out with a bang," said Ares with a grin while he was still wrapping Nyx's wound.

"Hey, Themis, can you tear up these three floorboards on the porch and put these three pressure plates in. Connect them to the two bombs, which should be placed in the center," said Ares.

Themis nodded and got to work as Ares finished patching up Nyx's shoulder. The two then went through the cabin looking for anything they could use and any other signs of people. They found nothing and almost no weapons, because Grandpa and the grandchildren had taken most of the weapons to the mountains. All three were outside now standing in a circle figuring out their next plan.

"Well, I think we'll be staying in the area for the next day or so to make sure if anyone comes back that they'll be murdered rightfully," said Ares.

"I think that sounds good. I'm going to need some medicine for this when we get back to the bunker."

"That'll be no problem. Just tough it out for the next few days while we wait. I'll let Eros know. His group is probably almost done prepping the bombs."

Themis planted the bomb, and the three of them headed back to the cabin they attacked a few nights earlier. The team planned to get a more secure rest there and wait for any troops to arrive, since a shift change was due.

"Success," read the message from Ares to Eros.

Eros, Tar, and Marshall were in their hotel room looking over the entire city of Billings from the sixth floor. Tar was in the bathroom planting a bomb in the ceiling tiles.

"Woo!" yelled Eros with excitement.

"You good, Sir?" asked Marshall who was sitting on the bed across from him.

"All cabins are gone and this is the last bomb we have to plant," yelled Eros with excitement.

"We're right on time and it's beautiful. The General will be very happy with us. How much longer, Tar?"

"Just a few more minutes, and we can get going."

"Good, because we needed to be out by eleven," joked Eros.

"Just think, Marshall, all of these bombs will go off in a week and you'll forever be remembered in U.S. history as one of the men who destroyed the Madison Legacy."

"It's one of the reasons I joined, Sir, and I'm happy that I'm doing something that matters."

"Glad to see your positive outlook on this, unlike when you first got here. You were a little shit when you got here but now you understand the bigger picture," exclaimed Eros.

"We have planted a bomb in almost every building here, and if there're any survivors, I am sure the debris smoke will kill them. You and Ares will also be sniping anyone escaping the city limits. The four of us will walk through with smoke masks and finish off people, too. It's just such an amazing picture that I might start crying," said Eros.

"Bomb's planted, Sir," yelled Tar from the bathroom.

Tar saw the garbage bags in the ceiling, felt the texture from the outside, and knew Julie was in the bags. Tar knew better than to cause a scene, unlike what Marshall would do, which was why he would not inform Marshall of how Julie was disposed. Tar felt disgusted but continued to remind himself he was doing this for his wife and would do anything required of him.

"Great. Let's get moving and get back to the bunker so we all can catch up on some sleep before the other three get back."

Tar and Marshall nodded and were ready to head back. Marshall had planted six different bombs in the city and would have full responsibility for the murder of these people. On the surface level, Marshall was coming across as loyal, knowing this was the way out of the military, while still making his mother proud.

Tar looked depressed and Marshall knew Tar was not a killer like the other members of the team.

"You good, Tar?" asked Marshall as the three left the room with their stuff.

"Yeah, I'm good. You good?"

"Yeah, just checking on you."

The three headed down the stairs to the bottom floor and Eros waved goodbye to the front deskman as the team walked out the door. The deskman waved back with a smile on his face and shouted, "Hope you enjoyed your stay!"

Marshall felt guilt emerge from his stomach. The bombs had yet to go off and guilt already resided in Marshall. Marshall felt that Tar was in the same situation of emotion and was only doing this mission for his wife.

"Thanks. We did," yelled Eros in an over-the-top happy tone.

The trio walked outside into the city. Eros spoke as they walked through the streets on the way back to the bunker. "Wonder if that guy's got kids? Seems like a very nice guy," said Eros who was joking about the man who was unaware he would be dead in a week.

Tar gave Eros a mercy laugh to decrease the tension as Marshall just walked onward with no acknowledgment whatsoever.

Marshall began thinking. Why does Eros act the way he does, and why does he need to be a cruel murderer? How do men like this come into power? Marshall put the pieces together as to whom the real bad guy was.

General Quartz was the main threat to people, and he had more Soldiers under his control than most armies. Marshall knew what he was doing right now would lead to a downfall of a nation. He believed Eros about the downfall that was soon to come. Ruthless people without a conscience win wars, while people who grieve are erased from history.

The three walked back to the bunker and headed to their rooms once they arrived. Marshall threw his bag on the floor and laid on his bed. Guilt would not let him sleep, but going to sleep was the one escape from what was inevitable.

CHAPTER 14

Hidden   *May 20, 2046*

The truck drove through the night. All of the kids fell asleep with Grandpa staying awake, constantly thinking about how dangerous and crazy Tommy really was. Grandpa was planning what he was going to say to Jerrod when they finally arrived home to their cabin. Jerrod was the only one who was starting to catch on to Tommy and realizing he was not just a shy kid anymore, but also a dangerous murderer.

Car rides were always relaxing for Grandpa. It brought him back to his years as a teenager, when he drove off to work, listening to his favorite music. He met Grandma at a friend's party, and he drove her home that night because she drank a little too much. That was when their love began. They both started singing passionately along to songs and that was when they both knew they were meant to be. Grandpa was excited to get home to tell her about this memory because the two of them loved to reminisce about their early days.

The truck pulled up about a half mile away from the cabin. Grandpa finally prepared what he needed to say to Jerrod as the truck came to a stop.

"Hey kids, we made it," said Grandpa in a soft voice trying to wake everyone.

Grandpa shook the kids who were half-asleep. The grandchildren slowly grabbed their items and bags. The sun began to rise, causing the woods to limit the visibility heavily.

Jerrod woke Natalie up with a kiss to the forehead.

"Wake up, Natalie, we're home."

"Ehh. Just five more minutes."

"We can go back to bed in just a little."

"Fine. I'll get up if you carry me."

Jerrod laughed and started unpacking the bed of the truck.

"Hey, Jerrod, can I speak to you real quick?" asked Grandpa.

Grandpa and Jerrod walked over to some trees that were to the side of the truck. Tommy stared at the two of them as they walked away from the group.

Tommy made eye contact with Grandpa and gave a deathly stare. Tommy was full of confidence after training and felt stronger than he really was.

"The rest of you should check all of the traps around the cabin because I want to be the first one to see Grandma," said Grandpa as he walked away from the group.

Omar, Natalie, and Tommy did just as they were told and headed to all of their traps and hideouts to make sure everything was in proper order. Jerrod and Grandpa walked toward the cabin as they spoke.

"Tommy's lost his mind," said Grandpa.

"He's gotten worse since the last time we talked?"

"He said things to me that I couldn't believe. He said he was going to slit my throat while I was sleeping. I don't want him in this cabin anymore. He doesn't belong with us. He's a monster. I know he's your brother, but he puts the rest of us in danger."

Jerrod's face was filled with fear while listening to Grandpa describe the horror story. Jerrod knew there was no way Grandpa could lie about Tommy in such horrific ways. Jerrod knew his Grandpa was telling the truth.

"What do you think we should do?" asked Jerrod.

"We're going to have a family meeting later this afternoon. We're going to address this and get all of the issues out in the open. If Tommy lies once during that meeting, then I'm kicking him out of the house. You, Natalie, and Omar are leaving for Madison soon anyway, and your Grandma and I can't take care of him by ourselves."

"What if I take him with us?"

"Tommy likes to hurt people, Jerrod. Tommy sliced Omar's arm two weeks ago and loved every second of the ordeal. He doesn't work well with others."

"I trust you Grandpa and will listen to whatever you think's best for him."

"I'll be sending him away, because he's a threat to everyone in the cabin, and I won't let him harm anyone else."

As Grandpa and Jerrod were finishing their conversation about Tommy, they approached the cabin. It was finally in sight.

"Well, you should go check your traps while I go give Grandma a good morning kiss because she probably hasn't spoken to anyone in the past two weeks."

"Yes, Sir," said Jerrod who left to go check his traps.

With the sun just rising, Grandpa did not see the cabin well. A smile grew on his face knowing he finally would see his wife again. Grandpa tried to hide his excitement, but his face showed all. Grandpa walked on the first porch step and took another step closer to the door.

At that moment, he realized the front door was shot open and heard a trigger plate release. Grandpa looked over to Jerrod who had his back turned to him because he was walking to his traps. Grandpa looked through the window to try to see Grandma one last time knowing this was the end.

A violent bomb went off, destroying the front of the cabin and smothering the area with fire. The cabin caught fire and started smoking. Grandpa was killed instantly by the explosion and was thrown twenty feet from where he was standing. The noise was just as loud as the explosions that went off at Whitehall six years ago.

Jerrod fell forward from the explosion and looked back to see what occurred. He saw his Grandpa's body laying lifeless on the ground in front of the cabin. Omar, Natalie, and Tommy all ran from their traps to check what occurred after they heard the horrifically loud explosion. All three of them feared the worst due to their recent combat training.

Natalie cried as she stood looking toward the cabin. Jerrod ran over to her, crying while they both hugged each other, trying to comfort themselves. Omar fell to his knees and cried, seeing his home of six years and his family burst into flames.

Tommy stood looking at the cabin trying to contain his excitement regarding the destruction that just occurred. Tommy was also happy Grandpa was finally gone and that no one knew what kind of person he was anymore. Tommy was able to be seen as the shy kid and not the crazy one anymore. Tommy did worry about what Grandpa had told Jerrod, but it did not matter at this second. He enjoyed everything happening and just wanted to focus purely on the explosion.

"We need to hide," said Jerrod sternly as he released Natalie from the hug and wiped his tears.

"That's the exact signal fire Grandpa was talking about in the mountains. Look at how much smoke is being released. Someone's coming to check this area. We need to hide right now."

Jerrod pulled Natalie away from where she was standing and into a nearby safety hideout.

"Stay in here, Natalie. You'll be safe. I need to make sure the others find a good place to hide, then I'll be right back," said Jerrod.

Natalie nodded her head and put the cover on her safety, hiding her from the world. She continued to quietly cry and tried to process what just happened.

Jerrod ran back over to Omar who managed to get himself to stand.

"What the fuck man?" yelled Omar who cried furiously and pointed to the cabin, which was now a complete fireball.

"We can grieve later, but right now we need to hide," said Jerrod in a calming voice.

"Let's just kill anyone that comes this way," yelled Omar.

"We don't know how many people are coming, and we don't who we're dealing with yet, Omar. Right now, we need to hide. We'll have plenty of time to fight in our life."

Omar knew he was right. He angrily walked away and went to his safety. He put the cover on his safety and sat there trying to calm himself.

Jerrod walked over to Tommy who was the last person that needed help. Tommy was not crying but just stood there, staring at the burning cabin.

"Tommy, you need to get into a safety right now."

"They're just gone," said Tommy coldly, showing no emotion.

"I know Tommy, but like I said to Omar, we can grieve once we're safe from whoever's about to come."

"I know," said Tommy who walked away to his safety, not needing any more comfort or support from anyone.

Jerrod stared at Tommy while he walked away realizing how right Grandpa really was about everything. Tommy had no emotion and did not care who was hurt. This was not the time to deal with this, though. Jerrod saw Tommy get into his safety and he ran back to Natalie's safety. He popped up the cover and fell into the hole with Natalie who immediately needed a hug. Jerrod put the cover back on and hugged her as tight as he could.

★ ★ ★

"We have a frequency change on a bomb at these coordinates," yelled Tar as he exited his room and entered into the center of the bunker where Eros and Ares were talking.

"Looks like I still have some job opportunities for you, Ares," said Eros.

Ares had a big grin on his face while he knocked on the doors of Themis and Nyx.

"Let's go, team. I need you two for a quick scout mission. Marshall don't bother getting up. You're not needed as usual," yelled Ares as he walked passed Marshall's door.

"I put the coordinates into your phone for you but you'll probably see the smoke once you get close enough," said Tar to Ares.

"Thank goodness we have such a useful nerd here," said Ares.

"Just remember that my kill count is still higher than yours," said Tar who reentered his room. Ares's smile shrunk because he knew that Tar was right.

Nyx, Themis, and Ares walked toward the ladder that led out of the bunker. The team had the coordinates, and the sun had risen. Stealth would be more difficult, but searching for the enemy became a lot easier. The team ran as fast as they could west to get to the cabin.

They saw the smoke in the air, slowed down, and returned to a crouched position.

"Oh, it looks like it was the family of six that got hit," said Nyx to the team.

"Let's hope the bomb didn't get all of them because I could really use some nice target practice for the bombs coming up in a few days," joked Ares, as Nyx and Themis both laughed.

"Yeah, you don't want Marshall getting more kills than you," said Nyx.

"Is that ever going to get old to you?" asked Ares.

"You know it never will."

The three continued west until Ares found a position optimal for him. Ares went into a prone position because he was now able to see the cabin and the surrounding area. The sun was out and bright. Themis and Nyx continued walking forward to get a closer look of the cabin and to search for anyone who was hiding.

Natalie and Jerrod were in their safety completely camouflaged from the surface. Jerrod and Natalie each had their preferred weapon as Grandpa had taught them to always have it slung around them. Natalie had her shotgun while Jerrod had his sniper rifle and pistol.

Omar remained quiet in his safety by himself but was armed with an assault rifle and had the gun pointed to the cover just in case anyone was coming. He was staying there until Jerrod told him otherwise.

Tommy had his own safety but was not trusted with a gun just yet. Tommy did have his scalpel, and he did have his garden knife. The knives may be no match for a gun, but they were better than nothing.

The Fairbank's truck was positioned a half a mile away with what was left of their ammo and other weapons. A good portion of their food was also sitting in their truck. Jerrod was hoping that whoever came would not travel that far west to find the truck.

Omar sat quietly with his tears finally stopping. He heard twigs crack. Omar immediately leaned further down in his safety so his gun would be perfectly aimed at anyone inspecting the area. It was taking Omar everything in his power not to throw the cover off and shoot the person above him. Omar knew this would get him killed though, and Jerrod was right. Today was not the day to fight these monsters. Today was the day to hide, so they could have another day to fight. With this in mind, Omar just sat there, waiting for Jerrod to give him the all clear.

Nyx crouched around outside, doing her best to be as quiet as she could. She did not see anything out of the ordinary. Themis was far away from her because he was inspecting another area. Ares had his scope on everyone providing them safety and the proper over-watch needed on missions. Nyx could not see anything and made it to the front of the cabin.

Nyx used her foot to kick over Grandpa's body, who laid lifeless on his stomach. With him turned over, Nyx could see his face was blown away and scorched by the flames. It was clear he died instantly.

Themis was not having any luck finding survivors while he walked through the area. His footsteps were noticeable to the Fairbanks; each knew when this man was getting close to their hideaways. The Fairbanks realized how poorly their traps were positioned because no one had triggered one yet. The Fairbanks were proud of the fact that their safeties were believable, as the enemy did not notice any of them.

Jerrod wanted to see his enemy and wanted to know whom he was fighting. He could hear such loud footsteps. He wanted to know what kind of person he would be fighting. Jerrod waited for the footsteps to quiet. Jerrod crouched up from his position and looked as if he was going to jump out of the safety.

"What're you doing?" whispered Natalie.

"I want to see what our enemy looks like so if we see them again, we can kill them for what they did to us."

Natalie's anger controlled her decision, and she agreed to let him look when she should have pulled him back for his own safety.

Jerrod popped the cover off slightly, to see a giant man walking away from the area where their safety was positioned. This man was the biggest Soldier Jerrod had ever seen. Jerrod knew he could shoot this man in the back but Jerrod also knew there was probably a sniper around because that is what he would do. Killing this one man would get the entire Fairbanks family killed. It was not worth killing the giant Soldier. Jerrod ducked his head back down and put the cover back on the safety.

"What'd you see?" asked Natalie who was curious and scared.

"A giant man. We need to hide as long as we can. I'm guessing they have a sniper in addition to the people walking around. We can't fight them now but I promise you we'll get them someday."

The two sat quietly waiting for as long as they could and hoped that Omar and Tommy would hide and not do anything stupid.

Nyx started heading farther west and alerted Ares she saw something.

"I see a truck."

Nyx approached the truck slowly and realized no one was in the vehicle. She saw a box or two of supplies and knew there had to be people in the area.

"Truck is stocked. People must have ran after the explosion."

"Torch the truck and supplies when we leave. Spend a little more time checking out the area, and then you and Themis can head home.

The three Soldiers spent the entire day looking in a mile radius of the cabin for any signs of life but found nothing. The sun was beginning to set.

Ares received a phone call from Eros.

"Find anything yet?"

"Nyx found a truck with some supplies, and we're torching it when we're done here."

"Good plan but torch the truck now because I need the team back here. There's a frequency issue with one of the bombs that Themis planted in town, and I want him to fix it. Themis and Tar will fix it in town tomorrow, and then we'll be all clear for the attack."

"Sir, with all due respect, I think they are hiding in the ground around here and I would prefer to stay here overnight to get any wanderers."

"Negative Ares. You're not spending the night out there alone. It doesn't matter at this point if they escape and tell others about us. The bomb goes off in a few days anyway and there's not much they can do about it anymore. Whoever's left alive is not worth our time anymore, so return once the truck is torched."

"Yes, Sir," said Ares as he hung up the phone and messaged Nyx.

"Destroy truck, head out," read the message from Ares to Nyx.

Nyx ran back to the truck with an incendiary bomb. Nyx looked through the two boxes and saw there was ammunition and some pistols in one of the boxes. Nyx threw all of the ammo to the ground knowing the rounds could go off in the fire. She did not want to accidently get hit by a random bullet. She kept the guns and food in the same spot she found them and threw the bomb at the truck. A small explosion occurred as fire engulfed the entire truck. Nyx watched the fire spread from the truck bed to the interior of the truck. The windows were blown out by the force of the explosion. The interior melted along with the tires. The smell of burnt rubber and metal filled the air. The truck was destroyed along with all of the weapons and supplies.

Nyx met up with Themis who was with Ares in his original position.

"Wonder why the dumb asses didn't take the truck once the bomb went off, if there were others," said Nyx.

"They didn't know which way we would be coming from so it was kind of smart actually," said Ares.

"By the way, Themis, your dumb ass didn't set the bomb in the city to the right frequency so you and Tar will be fixing that tomorrow. Got it?"

Themis nodded his head.

"Well, there's not much more we can do here, and Eros wants us back anyway. So if there's anyone out there, they better consider themselves lucky," said Ares.

"Yeah, they really should because I would have tortured them for that old hag shooting me in the shoulder."

Nyx, Themis, and Ares packed up their items and headed east back to the bunker. It was completely dark out, which provided great coverage for their walk home.

Several hours of night passed, and Jerrod stopped hearing footsteps. Jerrod was still worried if anyone was out there but it was time to leave this area. Jerrod opened the cover and signaled Natalie to follow him.

The two crouch-walked over to Omar's safety.

"Omar," whispered Jerrod.

Omar was wide-awake and was beyond relieved to hear Jerrod's voice. Omar lifted the cover off and peaked his head out to happily see Natalie and Jerrod crouched near his safety.

"Is it safe?" asked Omar.

"We're not a hundred percent confident but if we stay crouched we should be able to sneak into Billings to have a place to sleep tonight," said Jerrod.

Omar agreed with Jerrod and climbed out of his safety. Together they approached Tommy's safety.

"Tommy…Tommy," whispered Jerrod over the cover of Tommy's safety.

There was no response and fear controlled their imagination regarding what could have happened. Jerrod started to panic, hoping Tommy was okay. Tommy was Jerrod's brother first and no matter how crazy he became, nothing would ever change their relationship. Jerrod would always care about Tommy. This was what Grandpa had worried about the most over the last few years.

Jerrod lifted the cover off and saw Tommy was sleeping in the safety. Jerrod went to poke Tommy to wake him. Tommy woke up, started to panic, and took a swing at Jerrod with his knife, causing Tommy to cut Jerrod's arm. Jerrod's face was unrecognizable with the lack of light.

"Shit, Tommy, it's me so just relax," angrily whispered Jerrod.

"I'm sorry, Jerrod. I'm just scared," said Tommy convincingly.

"It's fine, but we need to move, so give me your hand."

Jerrod pulled Tommy out of his safety and then grabbed an old shirt to tie around the cut on his arm, controlling the bleeding. Jerrod did not know if Tommy meant to cut him or not. This was not the time to worry about this or cause a fight. Right now was the time to get everyone to safety for the night.

Jerrod walked toward the truck but saw the light of fire in the area.

"Looks like they found it," said Jerrod to the group with his hand pointed to the truck.

"Let's start walking to Billings and get a room for the night. The owner owes us a favor for the deer we gave him a month back. So it'll be free for us hopefully," said Jerrod trying to make everyone feel motivated to walk, when in reality, they just wanted to lay down and cry.

The Fairbanks walked toward Billings crouched, doing their best to be stealthy. They still did not know if anyone was watching them. Natalie grabbed Jerrod's arm to slow him down because she had something she needed to say to him.

"Grandpa was proud of you, Jerrod," said Natalie.

"He said he was proud of you every day. He loved you so much and told me you were exactly like your dad. He was so proud of you and was going to be so happy with whatever you end up doing to improve this world. You are important. Never forget that, Jerrod," said Natalie crying. She wanted to comfort Jerrod but did not know how.

Jerrod became emotional and a smile grew on his face.

"Thank you, Natalie," said Jerrod who gave her a hug.

"We need to keep moving, but thank you for saying that."

"No, thank you for keeping us alive because we need a leader like you for moments like this," said Natalie.

"Agreed," said Omar.

Jerrod gave a smile of appreciation but knew they had to keep walking, and the Fairbanks did just that. Billings would be their new home for the next few days as they planned their trip for Madison.

CHAPTER 15

Room Service   *May 20, 2046*

The Fairbanks ran through the night to reach the city of Billings. All members managed to avoid being seen by whoever was hunting them. Jerrod hoped they would be safe in Billing's for at least the night because the few members of the assassin team would not want to fight an entire city.

The family all relaxed when they saw the city, and all stood up from their crouched running postures.

"Let's get to the hotel, so we can catch our breath there for the night. Tomorrow we're making our move to Madison's wall," said Jerrod who was speaking to the other members of his family in a huddle just on the outskirts of town.

Everyone in the huddle acknowledged Jerrod, but were all tired from the day. The family did their best to fight back the emotions that were trying to explode out of their skins.

The Fairbanks family walked through town getting closer to the hotel. They passed the local pub, where dozens of people were having a good time, even though just out of sight, an entire cabin was engulfed in flames. No one paid attention in the Outliers because there was no sense of community. Madison was just as organized as the U.S. and citizens had their neighbor's backs when in trouble. That was exactly what the Fairbanks needed.

Jerrod walked into the hotel and was greeted by the owner who was reading a book at the front desk.

"Hey, Jerrod! What brings you in at such an hour?"

Jerrod stared at him with a look of despair as he and the rest of the family were covered in dirt, carrying their weapons, and each carrying just a small bag of whatever they could save during the attack.

"Our cabin was destroyed," said Omar who was standing behind Jerrod.

"What happened? Is everyone okay?"

"My grandpa and grandma are dead," said Jerrod coldly trying not to accept the fact of what he just said.

"I am so sorry....What happened out there?"

"A team planted a bomb on our house, and it went off killing our grandpa. We haven't seen our grandma, but we're guessing she suffered the same fate because they had to plant the bombs."

"Someone planted a bomb out here in the Outliers? Where would someone even find a bomb like that?"

"They looked professional. I only had a glimpse of one of them, but he seemed to be well-armed and dressed in black."

"That describes a lot of people in this area, Jerrod. Most people walk around with guns and dressed in black."

"Something big is about to happen. We're heading to Madison tomorrow, and I suggest you do the same. There's a reason they've been attacking cabins around this area."

"This is my home and my business, Jerrod. I can't just uproot and leave like that."

"Well, our choice was destroyed by whoever attacked us, and I'm sure your choice will be taken from you soon enough."

"Jerrod, can you just get the key so we can get out of here," said Natalie who was beginning to tear and just wanted to lay in a bed. It was clear to her that this man would not listen to Jerrod's advice, and there was no need to waste any more time.

"Can I get the key please?" asked Jerrod.

"Yeah, here you go, it's on the top floor. We're pretty booked tonight, so that's all I can do."

"That's fine," said Jerrod who took the key out of the front deskman's hand and began walking to the stairs.

The Fairbanks walked up the stairs and unlocked the door to their bedroom.

"I'll take the floor," said Tommy knowing he was going to have trouble sleeping tonight.

"Aww, I wanted the floor," joked Omar but caught himself because this was not a good time for humor.

Jerrod walked over to Natalie who was sitting on one of the two beds in the room, hugged her, and cried. Jerrod had kept his guard up for his family while they were in danger. Now they could relax. Jerrod let out all of the depression that had been stored. Natalie continued to hug him and started crying, too.

Jerrod and Natalie laid in bed together trying to fall asleep. Omar fell asleep, too, as he had just as long a day as everyone else. Tommy had a blanket and pillow set up on the floor. Tommy could not stop replaying the image he saw when his Grandpa was thrown from cabin by the explosion. The imagery was imbedded in Tommy's mind causing him to feel both heartbroken and intrigued by the whole ordeal.

Several hours passed but Tommy still could not fall asleep. Tommy realized this place had an operating shower, and Tommy thought that maybe a shower would relax him.

Tommy walked into the bathroom and locked the bathroom door. Tommy leaned into the shower to turn the lever. While he leaned into the shower, he pulled the shower curtain down on top of him along with the shower curtain rod. Tommy was mildly frustrated but just hoped he could get it attached again to the holes in the wall.

Tommy climbed on the edge of the bathtub to reach the correct height. Reaching down to pick up the curtain rod, he lost his balance, falling backward toward the door with the curtain rod in hand. The rod poked a hole in the ceiling tile just above him. Tommy was okay from the fall but looked up to see the damage he caused.

A smell of death came from the ceiling now that the tile was destroyed. Tommy used the curtain rod to poke the ceiling tile out of place so he could see what was there. Tommy saw a black rectangular shaped item and poked it to the ground. Tommy also felt something squishier in the ceiling and poked that down, too. A small garbage bag fell from the ceiling, releasing a stronger stench of death upon hitting the ground.

Tommy checked the garbage bag first. He flinched backward in panic when he saw two arms sawed off from a body inside the bag.

As panic disappeared, interest began to rise. Tommy decided to take a closer look. Tommy grabbed a hand towel and picked an arm up out of the bag. There was a lack of blood in the bag, which surprised Tommy, but he could tell that this arm was real.

Tommy sat there for ten minutes playing with the arm and cutting into the arm with the scalpel he always had on him. The arm grew old fast to Tommy because there was no emotion being distressed from cutting the arm.

Tommy put the arm back in the bag and tied the bag shut. Tommy moved closer to the rectangular black object.

Tommy noticed a light in the front of the item. Tommy put together what had just happened at the cabin and realized he was holding a bomb. Tommy once again began to panic at the thought of himself holding a bomb. Panic faded and Tommy's mind raced with different ideas for the outcome of this bomb exploding. Tommy thought of all the pain and emotion this bomb could cause. The only worry on Tommy's mind was he did not have control of this bomb. It did not seem like there was a way to turn it off or control the bomb.

Tommy put the bag and the bomb back into the ceiling. Tommy switched the broken ceiling tile with another tile, hoping no one would notice. Tommy traded the broken tile with a tile in the corner of the bathroom. Tommy put the curtain rod back on and started his shower.

Relaxation occurred within Tommy, but not from the shower. His mind raced with disturbing thoughts of what this bomb would do to people. Thoughts also raced about how those arms ended up where they were. Tommy imagined about the amount of pain this person experienced. Tommy's mind went blank about the events that occurred earlier and now purely thought of the items in the ceiling.

As the shower came to an end, Tommy realized that Grandpa spoke to Jerrod privately quite often over the past few weeks. What if Jerrod knew of his tendencies? Jerrod could tell Omar and Natalie and would not let him travel with them anymore.

At that moment, Tommy knew he was not going to tell the others about the bomb. If they were going to leave him anyway, there was no need to save them from this explosion if it were to go off over the next day.

The water stopped pouring out and Tommy dried himself. Tommy put some clothes back on, returned to the floor, and wrapped himself in his blanket.

"Hey, you good, Tommy? I heard some banging in there," asked Omar who was awake from the commotion in the bathroom.

"Yeah, I'm fine. The curtain rod fell, that's all," said Tommy calmly.

"Okay, just checking. Just know if you need to talk about what happened today, just let me know, Tommy."

"Thanks, Omar. I'm going to try to get some sleep now."

"Goodnight, Tommy."

Tommy did not respond while he escaped to a euphoric mind-state with everything that just occurred in the bathroom.

All of the Fairbanks slept through the night, knowing they had a long journey ahead of them to get to Madison.

★ ★ ★

The sun shone through the window, waking Jerrod. Jerrod looked over to Natalie to see she was still sleeping. Tommy and Omar were both asleep, too. Jerrod got out of bed and headed to the bathroom to get ready for the day.

A strange odor came from the bathroom, but Jerrod did not think much of the smell. His family was leaving in a few hours and would most likely never see this place again. Jerrod went back to bed and held Natalie as she slept, knowing how upset she would be when she woke up, knowing yesterday was not a dream.

Several hours passed and the whole family started waking. No one spoke while they just stared off into the room thinking of the events that had occurred. Tommy thought of the items in the ceiling. The destruction of the cabin was now in the back of his mind.

"Well, I think it's time we should get going. There's not much left for us here anymore," said Jerrod, sounding defeated.

Natalie hugged Jerrod tightly as he spoke while they laid in their bed together.

"We shouldn't warn these people about what happened last night?" asked Omar.

"You heard the desk man last night, Omar. Even if everyone here knew of an incoming attack, they wouldn't leave. This is their home and the only place they know. They would rather fight and die than find safety now to fight another day."

Tommy sat there listening to the conversation knowing there would not be a fight. There was going to be tons of explosions and then a cleanup team would come through killing any survivors. Tommy kept these thoughts to himself.

"Why are we leaving then? This is our home, and the only place we know."

"Taking a risk and failing is better than never trying at all. My dad said this to me all of the time, and I think that applies here. We could stay here until we die, or we can make a difference in Madison and save people that are willing to listen. It would be safer to just stay here and defend but that's not what Madison needs from us. They need us to travel there and help," said Jerrod.

Omar did not respond and simply absorbed the advice from Jerrod.

"We'll head south in a few minutes. The front desk man should have some maps we can use to look for some Outlier cities along the way."

The Fairbanks packed their belongings and headed down the stairs. Tommy felt upset with the fact he would never get to see these bombs go off, and he would never know what the story was behind the arms in the ceiling.

The four walked to the front desk where the man was sitting and reading as usual.

"How are you guys doing?" he asked with sincerity in his voice, looking up from his book.

"We'd like a map of the Outlier cities along the way to Madison," said Jerrod, ignoring the condolences that were given.

"Yeah, sure," said the front deskman who looked through his desk for the maps.

"Here you are. I wish the best of luck to you four on the trip, and I'm sure your grandparents would be proud of you for committing to the Madisons," said the man as he shook Jerrod's hand.

Jerrod shook his hand and walked out of the hotel. The Fairbanks remained quiet while they walked to the general store to buy water bottles. The family searched through the store and grabbed water and some canned supplies for their trip ahead. They did not have any money but traded the supplies for pistol ammo, which they had plenty of in their bags.

As Jerrod and his family packed the items at the counter, Jerrod saw someone out of the corner of his eye. A large man walking from the bathroom of the general store and out into the street. Jerrod knew that figure and knew that gear. The size of this man was uncommon for people out here, and Jerrod knew this was the man who helped kill his grandparents.

"That's him," whispered Jerrod to his whole family with a look of rage and revenge on his face.

CHAPTER 16

Stalked *May 21, 2046*

J errod watched the large Soldier walk out the door. His mind raced with war tactics and revenge, thinking of everything that needed to be done to accomplish this new mission that had just emerged. In just seconds, Jerrod had already created the plan he needed.

"Jerrod, what's wrong?" asked Natalie who saw the look of revenge on his face.

"You three head back to the hotel and get us a room again. We're staying and settling the vendetta tomorrow. Walk with me," said Jerrod without making eye contact with anyone as his mind could only focus on catching the Soldiers responsible for what had happened at his cabin.

The Fairbanks family walked out of the general store and headed east following the large man and another Soldier, who was normal-sized.

"I recognize that man. He was one of the Soldiers at our cabin. I'm going to follow him and figure out where their headquarters are. I want you three to head back to the hotel and get a hotel room again. We're staying here for a few days to catch these monsters then we can head to Madison," said Jerrod who was power-walking and doing his best to keep up with the men he was following.

"You're not following them into the woods alone, Jerrod," yelled Natalie who was starting to get worried because she had never seen Jerrod so intense.

"I'm quieter by myself than I am with a team. Please don't argue with me right now, Natalie. Just head back to the hotel, and I'll see you in a few hours. I promise."

Natalie knew there was no stopping Jerrod on his mission so Natalie stopped walking with Jerrod. Omar and Tommy followed her lead. Jerrod walked onward while the other three began to walk back to the hotel.

Omar put his arm around Tommy and Natalie.

"He knows what he's doing out there, and you know this so don't even worry about him. Just think, we get another night or two at the hotel," said Omar trying to boost the morale of the family, which seemed to be lacking.

Tommy was beyond ecstatic knowing they would be spending another night in the room with the bomb. A thrill ran through his mind of possible ways this bomb could go off and thought of all the people it could harm. His imagination ran wild as he continued to think about the bomb and the dismembered body hidden in the ceiling.

Natalie could not stop worrying about Jerrod. She knew Jerrod was a talented Soldier and a trained sniper, but he was no competition for a professional Soldier. She wished the best for him and tried to keep her emotions from controlling her reaction. There was no need to be upset yet because nothing had happened.

Jerrod followed the two Soldiers through town. They approached the tree line into the woods. More and more facts started to ensure Jerrod these two were assassins. The two did not even live in Billings. Most cabins in this area had been destroyed, too, and these two men walked confidently. Their stride made Jerrod think they knew they were the top predators in Billings.

Jerrod waited just a few seconds before following them into the woods, assuring there would be some distance while he stalked the Soldiers.

Enough time had passed and Jerrod headed toward the woods. Jerrod walked quietly and stealthily between the trees. He hoped he walked quietly enough to not be heard or sensed by the two Soldiers.

Grandpa had taken Jerrod hunting at least once a month for the last six years. Jerrod knew what it took to safely stalk and hunt an animal. He knew when to be quiet and when to make the move. If Jerrod were to shoot and kill these two men right now, there would be no chance of ever finding their hideout. If Jerrod shot the men right now, their entire team would know someone knew they were a threat. If they knew they were a threat, they would then abandon the mission or recruit more troops. That would be a loss for Jerrod either way.

Jerrod spotted the two men again, Jerrod needing to run to catch up to them. The two men did not seem to be speaking at all, just walking together in silence.

Jerrod followed for a little less than an hour and saw the two men stop at a tree. One of the men opened the tree trunk as if it was a door on hinges. He then knelt to the ground and pressed his hand to the vault. Jerrod was standing about thirty yards away and looked through his scope to get a better view. The two men had no idea they were followed home.

Right before one of the Soldiers headed down the vault, a man appeared coming up from the vault.

"You two are back already?" asked Eros.

"Yes, Sir. Themis properly armed the bomb, and everything is good to go," said Tar.

"Happy to hear it. Good work, Themis. Way to only need two attempts at running your phone past a black rectangular box. Real difficult stuff here," said Eros.

Jerrod was far enough away to be out of sight, but the Soldiers were talking much louder than they needed to be talking. It was clear they were way too comfortable in this area. Jerrod listened in on important information that could help him plan when he was going to do his own attack.

"Well, the General will be here in two days around noon. So, I guess we can pump ourselves up over the next few days and then finally attack this shit hole of a city that morning."

"Marshall still planning on leaving?" asked Tar to Eros.

"Yeah, the dumbass doesn't understand when he has a good thing but, hey, it's up to him. As long as he helps us on the mission, then I won't be pissed at him, and he can honorably retire his services."

"Well, Themis and I are going to rest up a little bit, and then we'll be back in the center room with everyone."

"I'm guessing Themis is the big spoon out of the two of you. I'm just joking, good work out there today. I'm going to get a little more fresh air, and then I'll head back down."

Eros climbed up and stretched as the other two men went down into the vault. Jerrod remained completely still until Eros climbed back down into the vault and shut the tree trunk door.

Jerrod knew where the attacks were coming from now. They had been hiding right under the families of Billings for far too long. Jerrod knew he needed to plan an attack on these monsters. They must have been living in the vault for some time now and probably felt safer than they should.

Now aware of when the final attack on the city was happening, Jerrod was able to plan when he should counter attack.

Jerrod took notes of the area and looked around for good spots to set himself up for vantage points. Jerrod also looked for different spots to set up spike traps and the safeties his grandfather had shown him how to make. He thought of where he could position Omar and Natalie and where they could be the most effective at shooting.

Jerrod spent about thirty minutes surveying the area. He spent the remaining time making sure no one was watching him before he moved. Jerrod felt safe and walked back into Billings. He paid extra attention to his surroundings because he needed to remember his way back for the counter attack.

About an hour passed and Jerrod knocked on the door to the Fairbanks hotel room on the sixth floor where they spent the previous night.

Natalie opened the door and welcomed Jerrod with a big hug.

"You were gone for too long, Jerrod."

"I know where they are attacking from now."

Natalie backed away from her hug because she felt how serious Jerrod was being, and she needed to hear what he had to say.

"They're launching an attack on the city in two days. I think we should attack their hideout while their attack is going on. This will slow down their assault and allow us to fight them on our time, giving us the advantage. There's not much we can do about them attacking the city so I think this will be the best plan."

Omar and Natalie looked toward the ground fearing their call to duty was now, and this was the moment that Madison needed the family. Tommy panicked that they would be leaving this hotel and getting a safe distance away from the bombing. Tommy started thinking of ideas and reasons for how they could stay.

"Any comments on this idea?" asked Jerrod.

"What will we be doing during this counter attack?" asked Natalie.

"I scouted out the area by their hideout and looked for the best place to set everyone up. We can also set up some traps to give us the best chance of killing these monsters."

"I don't want to go," said Tommy without confidence.

"We need you to fight for us right now, Tommy, and I can't leave you alone with the attack coming," said Jerrod.

"I'm not a good Soldier, and all of you know that," said Tommy trying to get empathy on his side.

"Now's your chance to become a good Soldier and make a name for the Fairbanks family. I'm attacking these animals in two days whether you're fighting with me or not."

"Well, I'm not, Jerrod. I'll be killed so fast, and there's no need for that. You three will do fine without me. In my opinion, we should just stay here and defend," said Tommy with the bomb on his mind.

"They're wanting people to defend obviously or why else would they take on an entire city? They have something up their sleeves, and we're not just going to sit here and wait for them to trick us. Let's attack them on our terms."

"I'm not going," whined Tommy.

Awkwardness filled the air as Jerrod grew angry with Tommy and no one else spoke. Jerrod felt confident this was the right choice for what to do next regarding this battle. He would not back down from this idea. It was clear that stubbornness was running through the Fairbanks family.

"How about I stay in the city with Tommy," said Omar with doubt in his voice, knowing that splitting up the team was not a smart idea.

"You don't want Tommy to be alone, and you want to attack these people, so I think this is the best solution. You even said today that a smaller number of people out there will be stealthier than a bunch of people. You and Natalie can kill them all if you have the advantage. She's great with a rifle and a shotgun, and you're a master sniper. You two are born to kill, and you don't need me out there," said Omar trying to plead his case. He felt sorry for Tommy who was admitting his fear and Omar just wanted to lighten the situation.

"You know we need you out there, Omar," stated Jerrod.

"I know you guys do. But you two will be able to kill efficiently without me though. I can protect Tommy and maybe even help this town if they rally against the attack. This is what will work best and what will make everyone happy."

The Fairbanks family grew silent again; knowing their time to prove themselves had finally arrived.

"All right, we'll split up for this attack, but I want on the record that this is a stupid idea," said Jerrod.

"Natalie and I will head to the woods tomorrow to begin setting up our attack in the area. We'll be digging spots for the traps and setting up in the trees for sniping opportunities. I want Omar and Tommy to secure yourselves in this building. You two are on the top floor and will have a great vantage point and high ground for any enemies that come your way. After Natalie and I kill all members of their shit team, we'll head back here and then finally head to

Madison with a great war story under our belts," said Jerrod who had motivation in his tone hoping to inspire everyone on this idea.

"I'm in," said Natalie.

"Me, too," said Omar.

"Thank you, Jerrod, for listening to me," said Tommy.

Tommy was able to fulfill his dream of staying in the area with the bomb to see it explode. Tommy now knew the bombs would most likely be going off in two days. This allowed him to properly plan where he would like to set up to watch the explosions. A benefit for Tommy was that Omar would be the one watching him and Omar was the most naïve, regarding Tommy's tendencies.

Jerrod looked toward Tommy who was enjoying this arrangement but could not stop thinking about what Grandpa said to him before he died.

"Hey, Omar let me talk to you real quick before I forget."

"Sure, no problem," said Omar as the two walked into the hallway.

Jerrod shut the door behind them and started to whisper to Omar.

"I need you to know something, Omar. Tommy's not okay in the head. He's crazy and he needs to be watched with extreme caution. Grandpa told me this right before he died. I won't be able to watch him when I'm gone, so I need you to make sure he's behaving and not acting crazy."

"I've been Tommy's roommate for some time now, so I think I know him the best out of everyone," joked Omar.

"Seriously, Omar, be careful. When Grandpa told me these things about Tommy, I'd never seen so much fear in his eyes. There's something seriously wrong with him, so please be careful around him."

Omar knew the seriousness of the situation now and agreed with Jerrod to be as safe as he could be when around Tommy.

Jerrod and Omar returned to the room and were welcomed by Tommy's glare of worry as Jerrod was acting the same way Grandpa did for some time. Tommy knew he just needed to wait a little bit longer and then he could unleash the inner demons inside of him. Omar was too nice to expect what Tommy had in mind for him. Tommy just needed to calm his excitement over the next two days.

The family spent the day together recalling memories of their grandparents, knowing that this would be their last night together for the next few days. They all laughed together at their stories, and even Tommy seemed to have lightened his mood. He still seemed to have something on his mind throughout the day. Nighttime approached, and this was the moment of action.

Jerrod and Natalie took a nap to get some energy for the next day or two in the woods. They would be digging traps and climbing trees so they needed as much energy as they could get.

Omar woke Jerrod and Natalie.

"Hey guys, it's time for you to be heroes," joked Omar.

Jerrod and Natalie woke up and gave their hugs and goodbyes to Tommy and Omar.

"We'll see you in two days. As their assault begins, you'll see a fire in the east. That will be us burning their bunker and hopefully the fire will catch the Soldier's attention. They will then head back to investigate and walk right into our trap. Just defend from this hotel, and don't feel obligated to be a hero. Madison needs us more than Billings so just remember that before you make any moves."

"Stop worrying, Jerrod. You're the one with the hard mission, so I wish you and Natalie the best of luck. Tommy and I literally will just be sitting here so please don't worry about us at all. Focus on your task at hand and complete your mission. I know you both are bad-asses, but now you just need to prove it to these assassins," said Omar to Jerrod and Natalie hoping to liven their spirits for their hard work ahead.

"Don't worry about us Jerrod, we'll be safe here. Just keep your mind on the mission," said Tommy. He was trying to come off as a good kid to Jerrod and the rest of the family.

"Stay safe, Tommy," said Jerrod as he and Natalie walked out of the door and headed for the woods. Jerrod knew Tommy seemed to be up to something, but there was no time for further exploration. Jerrod and Natalie needed to get to the woods and start digging so their plan would be ready in time.

"Well, they're gone now so I guess it's time to party," said Omar.

Tommy let out a small laugh, but then went to his bed and tried to sleep through the excitement of his plan to come.

★ ★ ★

Sun shone through the window on the sixth floor of the hotel but things were not normal. From what Jerrod had told his family the day before, Tommy believed tomorrow was the day of the bombs.

Omar woke up in a panic, realizing he was tied to the bed. His arms were outstretched and his legs were tied to the bedposts. Tommy had taped Omar's mouth shut and in doing so, he woke Omar. Omar yelled but the noise was muffled due to the tape. Tommy stood over Omar with a creepy smile on his face showing off how much he enjoyed the situation.

"I have to tell you something, Omar. I'm not normal. I have something wrong with me, and I just love seeing the pain through someone else. You have always been nice to me, and I thank you for that, but today I need you for this."

Tommy went into the bathroom, grabbed the bomb he pulled down the night before, and walked toward Omar holding the bomb.

"Do you know what this is? This is a bomb, and I'm pretty confident that it'll be going off sometime tomorrow. You'll be having a front row seat to this explosion, too. I'm leaving to camp out in the woods just south of here later today. It'll be a perfect spot to watch this bomb go off and watch this building collapse on you."

Omar was unable to understand what was happening. Just eight hours ago, Tommy was an innocent fourteen-year-old, but that mindset was forcibly changed now. Omar panicked because he could not move and was horrified by what Tommy was saying. Tommy placed the bomb on Omar's chest and watched Omar try to move away from the bomb.

"Before I go, I really wanted to try something out on you Omar, and I hope that's okay."

Tommy grabbed the scalpel from his back pocket, made random cuts all over Omar's body, and watched the pain in his eyes. Tommy continued for hours until he felt the need to leave and set up his camp in the woods just south of Billings. Tommy enjoyed himself even more than he thought he would and ended up staying much longer than he originally intended.

"Well, I guess it's time for me to get going. I'm sorry for you that this is how our friendship ends, but it's very exciting for me to see a friendship end like this."

Omar had passed out due to the pain he had experienced over the past few hours. The bomb still laid on his chest, and his body was covered in scalpel wounds that bled all over the bed.

Tommy left the key in the room and locked the door behind him. Tommy walked out of the hotel and headed to the woods with such a weight off his shoulders. His inner demons were satisfied for the time being, and a sense of relief engulfed his body. There was no guilt for what he just did to Omar. Only positive emotions came to Tommy after the events that had just occurred.

CHAPTER 17

Mission Elite   *May 23, 2046*

"Today's the day, everybody," shouted Eros in pure excitement as he knocked on everyone's door at four in the morning.

Everyone was already awake as this was the biggest mission any of them had ever done. No one slept well even if they wanted to act as if they had. None of them had experienced such destruction and all had some nervousness about what was to come.

Marshall laid in his bed staring at the ceiling, already dressed in his gear. His rifle and bag of supplies rested next to the bed. Today was his last day as a Soldier for the United States Army. Today was the last day he would ever have to kill someone due to a command. Marshall was not nervous about the act that was about to happen, but he was nervous about who he would be asked to shoot.

"Let's get going, Marshall. I need you to be positioned before the sun is up," said Eros through the door.

Marshall looked to the ceiling once more, knowing this was the last time he would ever see this base. Marshall stood up and while heading for the door, he saw the rest of his team putting on their gear. Ares looked pumped but Marshall could see it was an act and knew he was nervous about what was to come. Tar sat in the center room staring off into space with all of his gear. Tar would be running through the town with Eros, Nyx, and Themis. Tar was not as savage a warrior as the others were and seemed worried about being on the front lines.

"Now that all of you are out and ready, I want to give a final speech to you guys before we head to Billings. I want to thank all of you for your service for this country and know the destruction of Billings is needed for the union of the United States to occur. This attack is needed," said Eros while he primarily looked at Marshall throughout his speech.

"I'm proud of all of you, and you have all done outstanding work in prepping for this day. All of our work is put to the test today, and you all know the plan. So let's move before Marshall runs off on us," said Eros who sounded surprisingly sincere.

Marshall let out a small laugh and so did the rest of the team except Ares. Marshall loved the comradery that came with war and that would be the one thing he would miss the most after retiring. Marshall may hate and be disgusted by some of the Elitists, but knew they all had each other's back when the time was needed.

"Let's get going," said Eros.

All six members headed for the ladder and left out of the tree trunk. The members walked through the darkness at four in the morning.

Jerrod and Natalie sat in the trees with traps in the surrounding areas. They watched the team walk out of the bunker. They watched them head to the city. They could barely see the team as they were dressed in black and the sun was yet to rise.

"I think I only saw six people, Natalie."

"That can't be right. How do they expect to take an entire city with just six people?"

"There must be other bunkers," said Jerrod feeling defeated that his set up did not matter.

"I mean how else would they plan to take the entire city?" asked Jerrod to himself, feeling stupid for even thinking that this was the only hideout.

"You don't know there're others, Jerrod, so don't act defeated before you know the whole story. We have a mission to do so keep that in mind. We'll still plan this counter attack and kill whoever we can to avenge Grandpa and Grandma."

Jerrod knew she was right and refocused on his mission. He got his head back into the game again.

"After we hear the first shots, we will start the fire at their bunker. They'll run back to check what's happening. I'll fire the first shot, killing whoever I hit and then you follow up with a shot if you have someone marked. They'll then hopefully be in panic and run into our trap field."

"Yes, Sir," joked Natalie who was trying to calm Jerrod down but while still trying to keep his mind focused on the task at hand.

The Elitists reached the tree line of Billings before the sun rose.

"Ares, I want you setting up in the tallest tree on the east side of Billings that you chose on the scout mission the other day. Snipe any survivors that make a run for it and provide us some cover-fire. Marshall set up on the west side in the tree that you chose the other day and provide the same cover as Ares would."

Marshall ran through the woods to get into position before sunrise. Ares found his tree and climbed to the top. The other four Elitists waited at the bottom of the tree Ares chose, as they needed the sun for the next part of the mission. The team wanted daylight to arrive, as it would be easier to find runaways with the sun helping the team.

Tommy was positioned in a tree overlooking Billings to watch the explosions from just south of Billings. Tommy saw a man running through the woods. This man had a clear mission as he ran with confidence knowing exactly where he was headed. Tommy got excited knowing the bombs were to go off soon. Tommy looked to the hotel that housed Omar and knew pain was about to occur.

Marshall reached the tree he chose the other day. He started his climb to the top of the tree. The tree had thick enough branches so that Marshall could lay prone while still having a great view of the city. Marshall was told they planted bombs in every single building, but there was no way that a mind could fathom the explosion that was nearing.

Nervousness took over his mind and butterflies were eating at his stomach. Marshall had never experienced this level of nerves. Marshall had no idea of the kind of destruction that would be caused soon. He was nervous for the families living in this city and was nervous about the amount of guilt he would soon feel.

The sun peeked up over the horizon signaling the Elitists that the time they were all waiting for was now just a few minutes away.

Eros went to his phone and set up the screen to be on the right frequency as all of the bombs. All Eros needed to do now was push a button and the entire city would be in ruins.

"I am so excited," said Eros in a way that creeped out Tar.

"We finally get to destroy this shit hole and begin the next phase," said Eros.

Marshall saw the sun was rising, and he began to panic knowing what was about to happen. Marshall put his head down and looked through the scope holding back tears and doing his best to keep his mind on the mission.

It was now 7 AM and the sun was high enough to see any runners.

"Good thing I brought another pair of pants because I'm just so excited," laughed Eros. Tar, Themis, and Nyx did not laugh but looked to the city for the explosion.

"Ready to win?" asked Eros.

"Yes, Sir," said all three of them.

Ares and Marshall received a message reading, "Ready?"

Ares sent a vibration back to Eros signaling he was ready to fight. Marshall stared at his phone knowing that if he responded there was no turning back. Marshall decided to be a loyal Soldier one last time and sent the vibration, tearing up as he looked toward the city.

"Perfect," whispered Eros. He looked up to watch the city explode as he pressed the button.

There were a few seconds pause, but then the explosions started. Building after building shot debris in the air and covered the entire city with smoke and fire. The hotel was one of the last buildings to be triggered, but the team watched as each floor exploded causing the entire building to collapse. A deafening roar echoed from this little city in the middle of the Outliers. The noise could be heard from miles away. Each explosion built on another, creating the loudest and scariest noise anyone on the team had ever heard. Any army marching toward this noise would run the other way. This was the way to win wars and the United States understood that.

Screams could be heard from the survivors of this attack. Black smoke filled the skies, signaling the entire world that something horrible had just occurred. No buildings were left standing. All that was left were debris and people shouting in the streets. Thousands of people were killed within a ten-second window.

Tommy stared in amazement at what had just occurred. The entire city vanished in just a few seconds, leaving nothing but smoke and fire. Tommy enjoyed the screams and did not blink as the hotel, Omar was in, collapsed. Omar was dead, and Tommy kept replaying the day he had with him yesterday. Tommy had never been this happy in his life, and he did not have to hide his excitement anymore.

"What the fuck was that?" asked Jerrod who jumped in shock at such a horrifically loud explosion. The explosion shook the trees around them as if the trees were trying to escape the deafening roar. Smoke filled the skies where the city of Billings used to be. It looked like a volcano erupted with the amount of smoke pluming into the sky.

"Oh, no," cried Natalie as she put her hands on her face and cried.

"This is the only team. They didn't need troops because they had bombs. This is the U.S. at work right now. No one else could afford this many bombs," said Jerrod trying to piece together what has happening.

"You think Tommy and Omar are safe?" cried Natalie as she sat next to Jerrod in the tree.

"I don't know, Natalie," said Jerrod who hugged Natalie, but could not look away from the smoke cloud coming from the city.

Eros and his team waited for the debris cloud to settle before they entered the city to kill any survivors.

"Well, that was a fucking beautiful show!" yelled Eros in pure joy.

"Let's put our masks on and head into this masterpiece," yelled Eros who stood up signaling the rest of his team to fire and follow.

Eros, Tar, Themis, and Nyx all put their smoke masks on and headed into the city with their assault rifles drawn, ready to fire.

Ares saw someone trying to hold up his friend in the streets, but Ares shot the man in the chest causing him to drop.

"Already got one," read a message from Ares to Marshall.

Marshall stared at the city that was standing just minutes ago. Marshall began to shake in fear and shock because he knew he was part of the problem. He knew he was the reason these bombs killed all of these innocent people. Marshall looked down his scope to try to help his team and to kill survivors, but his conscience would not let him pull the trigger.

Marshall packed up his belongings and took his rifle with him while he climbed down the tree. Marshall stormed off into the west, not looking back at the city. Marshall wanted to do whatever he could to block this out of his memory. Marshall retired from the United States Military at that exact moment.

Ares looked for a response on his phone but received nothing and looked to where Marshall was positioned and saw no one. Marshall was not there, and the position was deserted.

Ares called Eros to let him know of the situation.

"Marshall's gone," yelled Ares over the phone.

Eros looked up to the trees and did his best to see him through the smoke clouds but did not see him.

"Catch him and kill him. I won't tolerate deserters on this team."

"You don't need over-watch, Sir?"

"These bombs did better than we thought. There are barely any survivors for you to shoot anyway, so we can just do the cleanup. I want you to kill Marshall, though."

"With pleasure, Sir," said Ares as he hung up the phone and climbed down the tree and ran west to catch up to Marshall.

Both Eros and Ares needed to make the assumption Marshall was escaping to West United States. He spoke so highly of retiring to places on the Pacific. The entire team figured that this was where he was running. No one knew who Marshall was in West U.S. He could have the perfect restart to his life without anyone knowing of his deserting history.

Eros looked toward Ares's position to make sure he had left and noticed a tower of smoke was coming from their bunker area. Eros looked at his phone and checked on the condition of the bunker. He was receiving an alert that there was a fire at the bunker.

Anger started to grow within Eros as so many different events were ruining this enjoyable experience for him. Nothing was going as planned, and this upset him.

"Hey, let's speed up killing these shits and then we can head back to the bunker to check out the fire," yelled Eros with disgust in his voice.

Themis and Nyx looked to Eros as he spoke but then returned to shooting the lifeless bodies confirming they were dead. There were almost no survivors and there was no one running away. All citizens were already dead or extremely hurt creating an easy cleanup for the Elitists.

Ares ran through the woods for about fifteen minutes doing his best to catch up to Marshall. Ares slowed down and looked at his surroundings to catch his bearings. He looked to the ground, saw footprints in the mud, and knew Marshall was not too far away.

Ares knew Marshall was a talented sniper even if he did not want to admit it and knew he had to continue with extreme caution.

Marshall knew he would be followed if he deserted and figured there would have been no easy way to retire from the U.S. Army. Marshall made some fake tracks heading in all different directions in the area that Ares was standing. The footprints all led in a large circle back to where Marshall had his rifle aimed. Ares needed to prove himself, but had been led into a trap. He had yet to realize it as he crouched through the mud.

Marshall had his scope on Ares who was crouched going through the mud following the footprints. Marshall was positioned in a tree just fifty feet away. Marshall went to his phone to call Ares.

Ares looked down to see who was calling and answered.

"Please head back now, or I'll kill you," said Marshall.

"You know you can't just desert the team and expect to not be followed."

"I get to retire after the mission today anyway, so why's it matter?"

"Well, honestly I always thought you were a smug asshole, Marshall, and I'll have pleasure in bringing your head back to Eros."

Marshall knew that Ares was never going to stop chasing him unless he killed him right here and now.

"Remember how you never went to stealth training with our class after graduating from sniper training?" asked Marshall, but Ares did not respond.

"Well, you've been following the wrong tracks for a few minutes now."

Ares looked up for moment, knowing he was in a bad position but stared back down his rifle. Marshall loaded the fire bird into his rifle and took aim on Ares's back.

"I'm sorry you're such a dick," said Marshall who fired his shot right into Ares's back. The bullet went straight through Ares causing the bullet to explode on his backside and travel through him, blinding him as the bullet hit the ground in front of him.

Ares knelt to the ground trying to keep himself standing but was unable to do so. He continued to fall over and landed face-first in the mud. Marshall waited a few moments to make sure Ares would not move and then approached the body. Marshall rolled Ares over to see his lifeless, burned out eyes. Marshall leaned into his body to take his phone from him.

Marshall called Eros, who had almost completed the cleanup with the remainder of his team.

"Ares? You kill the deserter yet?"

"No. Ares is dead, and I suggest you don't send anyone else."

Eros froze in hearing the news that Ares was now dead, and Marshall was still alive.

"Hey, Eros. The next time you hire someone, make sure they're not over-confident to a fault. Ares is great if you put him in a tree and tell him to shoot, but the second you ask him to stalk someone, its game over. He had the tracking ability of a six-year-old and is now dead."

"I'm coming for you, Marshall. Just know that because I'm coming for you right now. You're not heading home anymore. You're my next mission," screamed Eros through the phone.

"I'll be waiting for you," said Marshall as he hung up the phone and dropped it to the ground. Marshall started walking west and knew Eros would catch up to him eventually but he had a few minutes to calm himself.

"Ares is dead, and I'm going to avenge him," yelled Eros to his team.

"There's a fire at our bunker, and I want you three heading there now. You'll be able to take out whatever trash is there. I'm going to torture Marshall until he wishes he was dead and was still a part of this team," said Eros who started walking west out of the city.

Tar fired a question at Eros before he left.

"You want us to go in without any over-watch?"

"Well, I don't have any snipers left, so yes, Tar, I do."

Eros turned to Tar, grabbed a knife from his side, and held it to Tar's throat.

"Unless you want to desert this team, too, Tar?"

"No, Sir."

"Good, because I need you three to fix whatever's happening over there," said Eros who lowered his knife from Tar's throat.

"If you guys finish your mission before I get Marshall's head, I want you to come back here and wait for the General. He'll be here in a couple of hours with his team," said Eros who started to run into the woods.

Tar had no intention of checking out the fire but felt obligated because he knew Eros would kill him and his family if he were to say no. Therefore, he escaped his fear and walked east with Themis and Nyx.

"Let's go make the boss man happy."

"Is Ares dead?" asked Nyx.

"Yeah."

"I guess Marshall really was the better sniper out of the two," said Nyx to Themis who both smiled and continued with their mission in front of them.

Eros ran off chasing Marshall, while Jerrod and Natalie awaited the assassins to finally receive the revenge they deserved for what this team did to this community.

CHAPTER 18

Creating a Legacy   *May 23, 2046*

Jerrod was positioned in his tree doing his best to fight the tears after seeing and hearing the explosions from the city. He needed to focus on being in the battle and to think of Tommy and Omar later.

Natalie lit the tree on fire that hid the bunker. The two of them figured this was the best way to get the attention of the assassins. After the fire ignited, Natalie ran to the safety she had dug throughout the night. She had her shotgun aimed toward the cover and awaited a shot from Jerrod.

Jerrod looked into the distance waiting for someone to pop their head into his scope.

About an hour had passed since the initial bomb went off, and the fire had been burning the whole time, leaving clouds of smoke in the sky.

"Natalie, I see someone," whispered Jerrod from the tree to Natalie who was in a safety directly under the tree in which Jerrod was sniping.

"How far out?"

"A hundred yards give or take."

"I'm waiting until they get closer, and then I'm taking a shot. Be sure to leave the safety right after I shoot to hit whoever else is standing with them. It looks like there's only three of them. Either this is a small team, or they realized they didn't need that many people to deal with a fire."

"We'll kill whoever comes this way, Jerrod," said Natalie coldly, looking for a way to settle her vendettas.

"Oh, shit," screamed Tar as he saw his home for the past few months engulfed with fire.

"Stay tight team. Don't move out of formation. This could be a sabotage," said Nyx who looked down her scope searching for enemies.

Themis, Nyx, and Tar continued pushing forward but they had not seen any enemies yet. Jerrod was waiting for the trio to be right next to him when he fired so Natalie could pop out of the safety and get a kill, too.

The three Soldiers were right next to the tree that held Natalie and Jerrod. The Elitists had no idea of what was about to happen. Jerrod recognized

Themis as the large Soldier from a few days ago. He was going to be the first one shot.

Jerrod took aim at Themis and aimed right at his back as that entire team stared at the fire with their backs turned to Jerrod and Natalie.

Jerrod knew that once he fired, the other teammates would know where he was so he needed to trust that Natalie would fire directly after his shot.

Fear and nervousness were that last things on Jerrod's mind because he knew he needed to kill these monsters for what they had done to Billings for the last few months.

Jerrod stopped thinking and went into a war mindset. Jerrod took one more breath and fired his unsilenced rifle at Themis's back. This caused Themis to stumble forward and let out a manly grunt. He was unable to keep his balance. Nyx immediately turned around to see where the shot was fired from and took aim on the tree. She almost fired her first shot, but Natalie popped out of her safety and shot her shotgun with most of the shot tearing off Nyx's face, killing her instantly. Tar took aim at Natalie who was now completely exposed but Jerrod was faster on the trigger and fired at Tar, which hit him in the right shoulder. Tar panicked seeing his two allies were now dead. He ran east with a bullet in his shoulder.

Tar ran faster than he ever had. He dropped his rifle knowing there was a sniper in a tree and he needed as much speed as he could get. Suddenly, Tar fell, the ground underneath him gave way and his entire body crashed into a dug out pit. The pit was lined with four sharpened stakes. Tar was pierced by one of the stakes, going straight through his body. The stake went in just to the right of his stomach. Tar let out a horrible scream as he tried to process what had just happened to him. He was now unarmed and stuck in a pit.

Jerrod hopped down from the tree to kill Themis on a personal level. As he approached, Themis turned around and punched Jerrod in the face. Themis was still unable to keep his balance but cried hysterically after seeing his dead, faceless sister. Rage and sadness were empowering him to not give up and to not just lay down and die. Themis charged Jerrod who was still on the ground from the punch but was crawling away. Just as Themis pulled a knife to stab Jerrod, Natalie fired another shot from her shotgun, blowing off Themis's head. The giant's body went limp and collapsed to one side.

"Grandpa always said don't make shit personal when fighting, so if you have a clear shot, you kill this beast," said Natalie as she leant out a hand to pull Jerrod from the ground.

"You're right. I know."

"I think we caught the last one in a trap pretty close to us," said Natalie as the two walked east to find the man who triggered the trap.

They only needed to walk for a few minutes. They found the trap that was triggered. Tar laid there with a stake through his abdomen, drifting in and out of consciousness.

Jerrod sat on the edge of the hole and did his best to make eye contact with Tar. Jerrod tapped Tar on his face with his foot trying to get his attention.

"Hey, wake up, man. I have some questions for you," said Jerrod to Tar, before Tar passed out from the pain and blood loss.

"Just kill me already."

"I need your help with what just happened in Billings and then we'll kill you. Trust me."

Tar contemplated telling Jerrod of the horrific acts they have caused over the past few months. Tar continued to purely think of his wife while he faded in and out of consciousness. The only thing Tar wanted to do was head home and make sure his wife was living a happy and healthy life.

"Make sure Lily's okay," said Tar with a mumble that was barely understandable.

"What was that, Soldier?"

"My wife. Make sure she's okay."

"I can do that for you, but you need to tell me about this little organization you've set up here."

"We're a team of assassins, hired by the U.S. to destroy this city and the surrounding area," said Tar who coughed his way through this sentence.

Jerrod looked toward Natalie in fear, wondering why they chose their city for the target.

"Why here?" asked Natalie standing over the pit.

"Center between Canada and Madison. If you stay a little longer, you'll be able to see the helicopters come in with the troops and bombs. My team leveled the area for them to set up their missile launchers to attack Madison and Canada. If you stay too much longer though, you won't be able to find Lily for me in the States. Please find her and make sure she's okay. I've told you what you wanted, so please help me."

"How many troops are coming?"

"Hundreds upon hundreds of Soldiers. We're at ground zero for the next war. You two need to leave soon, or you won't be able to tell anyone. But I just beg you to find out about Lily for me. She's all that matters to me. She's my world," said Tar as tears ran down his face. His eyes closed for the last time.

"What's her last name?" shouted Jerrod in a panic now that he felt obligated to help because he spoiled the U.S. plans.

"Gollis," muttered Tar as his head went limp and his last breath left his body.

Jerrod looked to Natalie and saw that Natalie's eyes were tearing.

"He just wanted to get home to his wife," cried Natalie.

"It's the price of war, Natalie. He gave his life for his country, and we'll do the same for Madison to get the news out about these plans."

"What about Lily?" asked Natalie.

"We'll do our best to find her, but he just gave us a name belonging to a country we're not allowed to enter."

Natalie sat next to Jerrod who was still sitting on the edge of the hole and gave him a hug.

"We always have each other, right?"

"Always," said Jerrod hugging her right back.

"We lost so much, so fast over this past week, but we still have each other. We'll still help Madison in any way we can," said Natalie.

"That's the right attitude, Natalie."

"Let's go to Billings one last time, and then let's get moving south."

Natalie smiled in agreement and both stood up and began their final walk to Billings.

Nothing was said between the two as they had fears filling their minds. Natalie and Jerrod did their best to cope with the loss of their family and the city that had housed them over the past few years.

Both Natalie and Jerrod knew they needed to be in survival mode and be on high alert as they had just assaulted a squad of assassins. They would not be able to relax until they reached Madison. Knowing this kept the two of them lethal and the United States greatest enemy because they held the knowledge of the plan ahead.

Jerrod and Natalie walked to the edge of the tree line and looked toward the ruins that held a city just four hours ago. Natalie's tough war attitude faded as she collapsed to the ground, bawling her eyes out at the sight of this destruction.

Not one building was left standing, and the area had a creepy quietness because not one single person was in the city. Jerrod could not keep his fierce front on either and fell down crying, too, thinking about Omar and Tommy. The two cried together until they heard a noise they had not heard in years.

The sounds of helicopters got louder and louder.

"He was telling the truth," said Jerrod in surprise.

"We need to get moving, Natalie," said Jerrod with his voice becoming more panic filled.

Natalie wiped her eyes dry and stood. She looked up to see a troop-carrying helicopter fly slowly over the trees that covered them. A total of four helicopters flew over their heads. Natalie and Jerrod watched the first helicopter land and watched about fifty troops run out of the helicopter with masks on to protect themselves from the debris and smoke.

Natalie and Jerrod knew they could not stay any longer, even though all they wanted to do was shoot every last one of them. This was a battle they could not win and knew it was best to just fight another day.

Jerrod and Natalie ran south to Madison. They knew they needed to inform Madison of the attack to come but they had a long journey ahead. The distance from Billings and the wall of Madison was roughly 750 miles. It was going to be a long and dangerous journey, but one that was needed to ensure the U.S. never regained full strength of this land. Natalie and Jerrod were the last hopes for Madison, whether they knew it or not.

★ ★ ★

"Hey, Marshall, I'll be cutting off your fingers one-by-one the second I find you," shouted Eros in the middle of the woods, doing his best to find Marshall.

"Your mom was a giant slut," yelled Eros again with his words echoing through the silent woods.

"You're a bigger bitch than your mom for not coming to fight me," yelled Eros again as he did not know where Marshall was but knew he was walking west of Billings.

Marshall heard screams from Eros. He was positioned in a tree just out of sight of Eros. Marshall did not feel angry about any of the comments, because he did not respect Eros in the slightest.

"A monkey could snipe in a tree but give me a real fight, you pansy. You don't kill a member of my team and expect to just walk away cleanly, you dumb shit. How does it feel to be the reason the U.S. could lose everything? You messed everything up, you freak. I should be in Billings right now shaking the General's hand, but no. I'm out in the woods hunting your worthless ass."

Eros received a vibration from his phone and saw it was from Marshall.

"Drop all your weapons, and I'll show myself."

"It's a fucking deal," laughed Eros who dropped all of his gear with still no idea of where Marshall was.

"Let's fight one versus one with no weapons. Let's see who the real man is with no technology," yelled Eros.

Marshall climbed down from his tree and walked toward Eros who still did not know where Marshall was hiding.

"I could shoot you right now," said Marshall who was approaching Eros from behind with the scope on his back.

Eros looked at Marshall with a smile and walked toward him.

"If you were going to shoot me, you would have done it from the tree. I know you hate me enough to want to kill me with your bare hands. The feeling's mutual so let's get this started," said Eros, stretching and jumping up and down to get himself pumped for the fight.

"You're right," said Marshall who set his sniper rifle down and threw his pistol to the ground.

"I'm going to hang your head in my bedroom after this is over, you deserting piece of shit," said Eros as the two of them began to square off and got closer to each other.

Marshall remained quiet while he focused on fighting Eros. He knew we was stronger than Eros but also knew Eros had no issue with fighting dirty.

"You think you won't be caught for this? You and everyone you know will be dead after I tell the General what you've done here. Madison won't accept you because of Billings and the U.S. sure as hell won't want you."

"I guess I really do belong in the Outliers then," said Marshall with some sarcasm in his voice.

"I'll take you out of this world soon, so don't worry about finding a place to live."

"I hope you know news travels slow out here. Also, you should remember the winner of a fight is the one who decides how the story is told. That's how history works, and you should most definitely know this."

"You know I finally came up with a nickname for you," said Eros who was still squaring off with Marshall.

"Eris works perfect for you. She is the goddess of chaos and discord. Everything you have caused within the team. What do you think?"

"I think I like Marshall better."

Eros started to focus more on the fight and put his war face on to do what was needed to kill Marshall.

Eros threw the first punch toward Marshall's head. Marshall dodged the punch countering him with an upper cut to the jaw. As Marshall punched Eros in the mouth, it caused Eros to bite off his tongue. His tongue fell out of his mouth when he tried to speak.

"Hard to be an asshole without a tongue isn't it," joked Marshall who felt happy to know he would never again have to listen to his shitty sense of humor.

Eros's war face disappeared and was followed with madness. He charged Marshall with a flurry of punches but Marshall dodged every single punch he threw. Marshall caught one of the punches with his hands and tangled Eros up, but Eros head-butted Marshall in the mouth disorientating him and leaving him exposed to more punches.

Eros threw a hard right hook sending Marshall to his knees. Marshall immediately went back to his feet with his fists raised. Eros smiled at Marshall, after winning that exchange with blood pouring through his teeth.

Eros had unearned confidence at this point and decided to jump right back into a flurry of punches. Marshall dodged the punches again and hit Eros with an uppercut in the same exact spot as earlier causing Eros to back up, needing to regain his composure.

Eros knew he was losing this fight and had extremely underestimated Marshall's hand-to-hand combat. Eros grabbed a knife hidden in his vest and charged Marshall with his arm extended.

Marshall grabbed the wrist holding the knife. His left hand disabled the immediate threat and followed up with a right jab to Eros's throat. The punch shocked and disoriented Eros. Marshall took his right hand and punched just above Eros's forearm causing his entire arm to give way. Marshall then pushed Eros's wrist, which was holding the knife, into Eros's chest. Eros fell straight on his back with the mass amount of force Marshall used to push the knife into Eros. The knife now stuck out of his chest. Blood flowed from his chest, and his mouth continued to bleed from biting off his tongue.

"The Elitists are over," said Marshall as he ripped the knife out of Eros's chest and went to grab his gear.

Marshall grabbed his pistol and walked back over to Eros, who was squirming on the ground. He fired a shot into Eros's head with no hesitation or final words. Marshall knew Eros had been living on this planet far too long and felt he did not deserve one more second.

A new chapter had just opened for Marshall as he continued walking west, creating a larger gap from his previous lifestyle. Marshall felt more at ease with every step he took closer to the Pacific. He knew he would not be told to kill again.

CHAPTER 19

My Enemy   *May 23, 2046*

The air was more refreshing than ever today. Marshall woke up the past few weeks inside an underground bunker, but today was different. No one knew where he was and no one was barking orders at him. Marshall was heading to West U.S. to start a new life. General Quartz may be looking for Marshall but information traveled slowly in the Outliers so Marshall was not worried yet.

Marshall had his sniper rifle on his back and proudly walked through the woods. Many different emotions went through his mind. This was the first time he was free to act in the way he pleased. Marshall had constant mental battles with himself over the past few weeks regarding what was right and wrong and what needed to be done. Marshall finally settled his internal disputes and accepted the person he was.

Marshall knew he made his mother proud by killing Madisons for so long and helping the U.S. win so many battles over the years. He felt his mother was proud of him and she could finally rest in peace now that Marshall was retiring from the war.

The United States could be content with the mission he just accomplished. Marshall also gave himself mental compliments thinking that killing Ares and Eros was bettering the United States. The U.S. will be better without those killers leading troops to be murderers, too.

Ariel could be happy because she would finally see the Pacific coast through Marshall's eyes. She could live in a house with Marshall even if she was not physically there. Her idea of freedom sprouted Marshall to be the man he was right at this moment.

The one issue Marshall was working to overcome was trying to justify the death of the city of Billings through the Outlier's eyes. There were two sides to every story and Marshall had yet to determine what the benefits were for Billings after the bomb. He knew this would eat at him every night until he could mentally justify what he did. Luckily, Marshall had a long walk toward West U.S., so he had an abundance of time to play out different ways of looking at this issue.

"Help!" shouted a kid from the distance who was limping toward Marshall.

Marshall readied his pistol, not trusting anyone out here and still being on high alert from the past destruction. Marshall took aim at the kid.

"Stop moving. What's your name?"

"It's Tommy, please don't shoot," shouted Tommy with fear in his voice.

"I was at the bombings earlier today. Please help. There're a bunch of troops searching the area and killing people," cried Tommy.

"Sit down and let me look at your leg. We're pretty far away from the bombings so they shouldn't clear this far out. Where're your parents?" asked Marshall as he holstered his pistol and approached Tommy who was now sitting on a fallen tree.

"They died in the explosion," said Tommy coldly, unable to make himself cry.

Marshall felt even more guilt, and his mental battle worsened. Trying to compensate the bombings was now even more difficult.

"I'm sorry to hear that, Tommy," said Marshall with defeat in his voice. Marshall tied a bandage around Tommy's leg, which seemed to have been sliced by a knife.

"What're you doing out here?" asked Tommy.

"I was on a hunting trip over the past few months, but I'm returning home to West U.S. right now."

"Please don't leave me alone out here," begged Tommy.

Marshall realized this was the moment he could use to defeat his guilt about what had occurred. Marshall could save this kid's life. It would not equal the damage he caused, but it could help him just enough to sleep at night.

"Do you want to come with me to West U.S.?"

"I've never been out of Billings. Will they allow me in there? I don't even know your name, sir."

"My name's Marshall, and I'll make sure you'll be able to get in Tommy. I promise you that. I'll take care of you."

Tommy gave Marshall a smile while Marshall awkwardly looked down at the leg he was fixing. Marshall did not know what to say.

Tommy's leg did not hurt as much as he pretended. Tommy saw Marshall walking through the woods about a quarter mile back and planned a way to get to speak to him and not come off as a threat. Tommy knew Marshall was not a hunter because the rifle he was using would destroy the animal, leaving the carcass inedible.

Tommy had his scalpel in his back pocket and the garden knife in his other pocket. Now that Tommy was away from people who knew of his troubled mind, he could play off the innocent kid until he found himself in an opportune moment to attack.

Tommy imagined the look on Marshall's face if he grabbed the knife in his pocket and sliced his throat right here and now. Tommy knew he needed Marshall alive though to survive the journey. This alone was the only reason Tommy had not attacked at that very moment. Tommy dreamed of stabbing Marshall while he slept but did his best to keep his inner demons under control.

Marshall looked up at Tommy thinking this was opportunity telling him now was the chance to make peace with the Outliers and other enemies. Now was the time to live a less war-filled life.

"How's your leg feel?"

"It feels better, Marshall. Thank you for doing this for me. You really don't mind if I tag along with you to the States?"

"Not at all Tommy, I feel responsible for you right now and there must be a reason we met in the middle of the woods like this. I want to help you, Tommy."

The two began walking west and Tommy stopped limping as much as time continued. Marshall had Tommy walk in front of him so Marshall would not walk too fast for him. Tommy agreed and both continued onward.

Marshall saw a shiny reflection come from the back of Tommy's pants and it seemed like it was a knife. That in itself was not odd as they were in the Outliers, but Marshall did find the cut on his leg to be a perfectly straight line. Tommy stopped limping almost completely, too. Tommy showed almost no emotion since speaking of his parent's death. Marshall was a mess after the explosion that killed his mother. Marshall thought of why this kid would lie to him but could not think of a valid reason.

Marshall laughed to himself and thought how crazy war had made him. He was unable to trust a kid but knew he had to try to trust him because there was no reason to not trust Tommy.

Tommy continued walking west recreating different scenarios in which he could attack Marshall and continued planning how long he would need Marshall. The pain coming from Marshall's screams while cutting into him, filled Tommy with joy, but he knew he had to act at the right time.

Neither of them really knew who the other person was, but it did not matter. One was trying to leave a past of murder and destruction behind, while the other was looking to continue his assault on the world.

"Hey, can we stop to eat soon?" asked Tommy.

"No problem, Tommy. I got some canned stuff if you'd like," said Marshall.

"Yeah, that sounds good, Marshall..."

June 6, 2046

"Sir, I found him. I found the Captain of the team," rang a Soldier over the phone to General Quartz. General Quartz looked to his feet in shame that five out of the six members of the Elitists were now dead.

Quartz sat in large tent on top of the now-vanished city of Billings. The opening of the tent was missing and he looked over his makeshift empire. The tent city held about 300 troops all in group tents. The troops spent all hours of the day and night guarding the area; hunting scouts from other cities, and most importantly, building the launching device.

In Quartz's tent, there were dozens of chemical warfare experts and missile specialists. Their job was to create a missile filled with the same gas that destroyed the majority of the world two decades ago. The targets were Madison and Canada. Communication was not capable of traveling very far, which allowed Quartz to take his time in the set up and plan the attacks perfectly.

A troop ran into Quartz's tent and briefed him on his mission to find the Elitists.

"I'm sorry, but our team is still unable to find the last man, Sir."

"That's all right Soldier. I don't think this one's dead," said Quartz who stood up from his seat and signaled the Soldier to take a walk with him.

The two walked through the tent town together.

"Before the bomb went off, Eros, the Captain of this team, messaged me, alerting me that Marshall, the man you can't find, wanted to quit this mission. Eros agreed and told him he could retire once the city was gone, and he did proper over-watch. Marshall did not do this as Eros sent me a message just an hour before we arrived saying that there was an issue. I think Marshall killed my team. That's unacceptable. No Outlier could kill Eros with a knife wound but Marshall was a talented Soldier, and I wouldn't be surprised if he did."

"What should we do, Sir?"

"I want you and some Soldiers of your choosing to head to West U.S. and find this man for me. The bodies were found west of here so that's our only lead. No one will know he's a traitor. There's no way of knowing that because no one even knew this mission existed."

"I'll get moving right away, Sir."

The two climbed two flights of outdoor stairs surrounding the frame of the missile launcher. The missile launcher was about twenty feet tall and centered in the middle of their tent town. The missiles themselves were being worked on in other tents and were not ready for the final deployment.

"This machine will be up and running in two months' time, so I would like to get confirmation that this man is dead before the attacks start. Marshall was not on board for mass killings, and he'll most likely feel guilty as time goes on and will try to stop this mission. That can't happen, so I would love if you could bring me his head as soon as possible," said Quartz who stared at the Soldier. The General signaled him with his eyes that he wanted the Soldier to move right this second.

"Yes, Sir," yelled the Soldier.

The Soldier ran to his tent and looked for fellow Soldiers who would be a good fit for this hunt and kill mission.

Quartz looked up to the sky knowing that victory was just a mere few months away and he did not want any loose ends going forward. Marshall must be killed to ensure the privacy of this mission. Little to his knowledge, Jerrod and Natalie were closing in on the Madison's wall and they would soon create a new threat to General Quartz.

CPSIA information can be obtained at www.ICGtesting.com
Printed in the USA
LVOW12s0321250216

476642LV00003B/185/P